I0714229

Miles

TWILIGHT FALLS BOOK SEVEN

A.M. SALINGER

BOOKS BY A.M. SALINGER

NIGHTS

One Night - 1

The Escort - 2

Tokyo Heat - 3

Sweet Obsession - 4

Sweet Possession - 5

The Proposition - 6

Undisclosed - 7

Hush - 8

One Day - 9

TWILIGHT FALLS

Alex - 1

Carter - 2

Hunter - 3

Wyatt - 4

Drake - 5

Tristan - 6

Miles - 7

CHAPTER ONE

MILES MARTINEZ PULLED UP OUTSIDE A CHARMING, white clapboard house in a quiet suburb in Twilight Falls. Warm lights brightened the multi-pane, sash windows, their glow complementing the festive decorations adorning the facade and porch, and strung prettily on the bushes and moss-draped oak trees framing the property.

It was almost Christmas.

Miles turned into the drive and parked between a pickup and a Jeep. A wave of melancholy danced through him when he stepped outside and studied the Batistas' home.

He used to come here every Wednesday night, before the accident. Despite the Terrible Seven's reputation, Helen Batista had loved nothing more than cooking meals for her son Wyatt's friends. They had been renowned troublemakers since childhood, tales of their misdeeds spreading far beyond the town where they had grown up.

A wry smile stretched Miles's lips.

Old man Coulton must be glad we're all grown up.

Gary Coulton had been the sheriff when the Terrible Seven begun earning their unsavory prestige. Miles had heard he would soon be retiring. As for Wyatt's parents, they had moved to Utah several years ago.

It was just several of the changes Miles had woken up to when he'd emerged from his twelve-year-long coma two months ago.

So much happened while I was sleeping.

His chest tightened. He took a deep breath and squashed the dismal feelings threatening to overwhelm him. He couldn't let his mood ruin poker night.

The front door opened as he headed up the porch steps.

A pretty brunette with green eyes appeared.

Izzy Batista, Wyatt's younger sister and the unofficial eighth member of the Terrible Seven, smiled at him warmly. "Hey."

"Hi, Izzy." Miles kissed her cheek and glanced at the pickup. "Wasn't Tristan going to L.A. this week to visit James?"

"James came over." Izzy made a face. "Which means there are currently four horny men in my kitchen wondering when dinner and poker is going to be over so they can rush home and have monkey sex."

"I heard that," a handsome man with dark hair and glasses snapped as he crossed the hall behind her. "And Nathan's here, so that's six horny guys under your rooftop." The corners of his mouth lifted as he looked at Miles. "Hi, Miles."

"Hi, James."

James Lang was Tristan Hart's fiancé. Not only was he the manager of Crazyknot, a world famous rock band that regularly sold out concerts wherever they played, he was also best friends with Roman Campbell, Crazyknot's front man and the guy Drake Jackson had surrendered his closely guarded heart too.

Izzy studied Miles's SUV. "You getting used to your new ride?"

Miles heard the unspoken question in her voice. He'd shocked his mother and his friends when he'd said he wished to drive again. They'd all assumed he would be too traumatized to want to get behind the wheel of a vehicle so soon after coming out of the coma.

Miles had to admit he'd not been too crazy about the idea at first either. But he was determined to pick up the pieces of his broken life. Gaining his independence had been the first step toward achieving that goal.

He'd been nervous as hell the first few times he'd gone out in Elaine Martinez's Chevy. It was only because one of the Terrible Seven always insisted on being with him on the drive that he'd managed to overcome his fears and recover his confidence.

Miles smiled and finally answered Izzy's question. "It's like a riding a bike."

She sniffed. "Yeah, well, they say that about sex too. Considering I haven't had a date in over a year, I think

I'm gonna forget how to do the boogie-woogie in the sack."

Miles choke-laughed on his spit.

He'd forgotten how brazen Izzy was. Considering she'd firmly foisted herself in her brother's circle of friends when they were still in middle school, he shouldn't have been surprised by the woman she'd grown into.

Miles hoped the low light masked his reddening ears as they headed inside the house. He was willing to bet Izzy had a good deal more experience when it came to sex than he did.

A memory had him grinning.

"You still have that picture of Carter you took in the boy's locker room in high school?"

Izzy flashed an evil smirk at him over her shoulder. "You mean the one with his naked behind on full display? You bet I do."

Miles was still chuckling to himself when they entered the kitchen. His stomach twisted a little at the sight of Drake and Roman chatting as they made a potato salad.

Drake brightened when he saw Miles. "Hey." He came over to hug him.

Miles stiffened slightly before relaxing in his hold. "Hi."

For once, the smile he gave Drake and Roman was as genuine as the ones they offered him. It had been especially hard for him to accept that Drake was engaged and would soon marry Roman. But he couldn't deny the truth before his eyes: the two men were clearly crazy about each other.

It's just one more thing I'll have to come to terms with.

Tristan waved a spatula at him where he was cooking steaks at the range. "Want a soda?"

"I'll get it." Miles took the drink out of the refrigerator. He looked around curiously. "Where's Wyatt?"

"He was here a minute ago," Izzy muttered.

"Ten bucks says he and Nathan are making out in the den," James drawled where he handled the fryer.

Roman grinned.

Wyatt and Nathan Hardy returned looking suspiciously flushed just as Izzy took a tray of freshly baked bread out of the oven. The rest of the Terrible Seven turned up with their partners before she could tell her brother and his fiancé off.

The only one missing was Carter Wilson. The Hollywood movie star was on a shoot in Europe. His husband Elijah came with their adopted daughter Maisie instead.

"Is this really going to be Carter's last movie?" Finn West asked curiously.

Elijah made a complicated expression as he cut Maisie's meat. "Yeah. It was the last project he was contracted to do before the whole scandal with Mira broke out. He'll be starting his role as an executive producer in the New Year."

Izzy and the others had brought Miles up to speed with the major events he'd missed over the last twelve years so he knew about Carter and Mira Peters, the movie producer who'd disgraced herself after she'd attempted to blackmail Carter into resuming the affair they'd had at the start of his career.

Miles still found it hard to believe that the Carter Wilson he knew had become a world-renowned actor. To him, Carter would always be the cheeky boy with hazel eyes and a dazzling smile that almost always got him out of trouble.

Hunter Thomson stole a fry from Theo Miller's plate. "I bet his legion of fans aren't happy about that. Carter is ridiculously popular with guys and gals." He pointed the thin strip of fried potato at Elijah. "You might get hate mail."

Roman snorted. "Between Carter and *La Petite Bouche Gourmande,* I'd choose Elijah's cakes any day."

"Yeah, I think Elijah's safe," Alex Hancock-West drawled. "Besides, he's just as stunning as Carter. I'm surprised Carter doesn't get hate mail for having laid claim to California's hottest pastry chef."

Elijah flushed at their grins.

"I'm gonna marry Papa Elijah when I grow up," Maisie said confidently.

"I thought you were planning on marrying your Uncle Miles," Izzy reminded the little girl drily.

Miles blinked, nonplussed. "She is?"

"Yup." Drake took a swig of his drink. "The kid made the declaration at your homecoming party, just before you got there."

Maisie squirmed in her chair and bit her lip. She

leaned closer to Elijah. "Can I marry you both?" she whispered.

Elijah's mouth pressed to a trembling line as he pretended not to laugh. "I don't think that's going to be possible, sweetheart," he said in a strangled voice.

Maisie's face fell. She squinted at Miles.

"Wait for me, Uncle Miles."

Miles bit the inside of his cheek hard as Elijah's expression fell. Izzy and Roman's shoulders quivered.

"Congratulations." Tristan patted Elijah's back. "Your daughter just dumped you."

Theo sighed when Hunter swiped more fries from his plate. "You know, you're acting like I don't feed you."

"Oh, you feed me well." His fiancé chomped down on a fry, licked his fingers, and arched an eyebrow. "Why, last night you stuffed me so good I—"

Theo hastily clamped a hand over Hunter's mouth. Izzy's grin transformed into a scowl. Wyatt sighed. Finn hid a smile in his beer.

"Is Uncle Hunter being rude again?" Maisie asked curiously.

"You don't know the half of it, kid," Drake grunted.

"You should put a muzzle on him," James told Theo.

Hunter's eyes brightened with a wicked light. Theo groaned.

"I think you just awakened his inner beast," Nathan chuckled.

The conversation soon shifted to Christmas plans.

Alex and Finn had invited all of them to their place.

It was big enough to host a huge party and they had enough room to accommodate everyone for the night.

"Is Elaine going to be in Singapore for Christmas?" Izzy asked Miles.

"Yeah," he replied lightly. "She's not back until the New Year."

It had taken a lot to persuade Elaine to go on a well-deserved holiday. In all the time Miles had been in a coma at the Sunrise Care Home, she'd stayed by his side and came to see him every day, just as Izzy and the Terrible Seven visited every week. Miles had spoken to his mother's closest friends and finally convinced Elaine to go on a cruise with them.

"We'll miss her at Christmas," Alex said quietly. "But I'm glad she's gone on that trip."

Izzy and the rest of the Terrible Seven were all close to Elaine. She'd been a quasi-mother figure to them ever since she'd adopted the gang of misfits when they were kids.

Miles forced his face to stay relaxed.

The happy hours all of them had spent at his home felt like a lifetime ago. A lifetime he would never recover.

It wasn't until they'd finished their game of poker, which James won by a landslide to a roar of groans and Tristan's satisfied grin, that Miles took the opportunity to slip outside while his friends cleared the table and Wyatt and Nathan made coffee for everyone.

He settled on the porch swing and looked out over the twinkling lights in the distance. The Batistas' home was on a low hill overlooking the valley that cradled Twilight Falls.

Miles's shoulders slowly unknotted as he gazed blindly at the town where he'd grown up. A wave of guilt welled up inside him.

I'm such a loser.

CHAPTER TWO

MILES KNEW HE SHOULD BE HAPPY FOR HIS FRIENDS. AND he was.

But he was also irritated and miserable and just plain…lost.

It wasn't just because he'd woken up in a stranger's body. He felt like an outsider within the circle of people he was once closest to. And he didn't know how to fix that.

The wind picked up, rustling branches and scattering the dead leaves on the lawn. It brought a chill that raised goosebumps on his skin.

Miles was rubbing his arms and wishing he'd taken his jacket from the coat rack when Izzy came out of the house with a couple of blankets. She sat beside him and gave him one.

"Thanks," Miles murmured gratefully. He wrapped the blanket around his shoulders.

"What's wrong?" Izzy said after a while.

Miles wasn't fooled by her quiet words. She was

giving him a look that seemed to see straight through him. He lowered his gaze and cut his eyes to the lights of the town.

"What makes you think there's something wrong?" he said, keeping his voice light.

"Because I know you better than you know yourself."

Something in her tone made his head swivel. He stared at her.

Izzy's eyes had darkened with an unnamed emotion. She worried her lip with her teeth.

"Are you still seeing the psychologist?"

Her question made his jaw tighten. Whatever Izzy saw in his face didn't deter her one bit.

"You know she said you'll feel all kinds of emotions for a while and you should—"

"I'm okay, Izzy," Miles said more forcefully than he'd intended.

Izzy furrowed her brow. She jutted out her chin. "No, you aren't."

Miles's nails dug into his palms.

Izzy sighed when she saw the movement. He stiffened when she took hold of his hand and clasped his fingers.

"You're not okay, Miles," she said softly. "And no one expects you to be. The guys in there?" She glanced at the bright window behind her.

Miles followed her gaze.

Elijah had changed Maisie into her pajamas and Tristan was reading a story to the sleepy little girl.

"They all know that. And they're here for you. *I'm*

here for you." Izzy's fingers tightened around his. "You will be okay, Miles. Just…give it time."

Miles swallowed past the sudden lump in his throat. His vision blurred with unshed tears as he gazed out into the night, grief at all that he had lost choking his breath. Izzy leaned against him and dropped her head on his shoulder, her quiet presence a balm on his conflicted heart.

By the time they went back inside the house, Miles was more composed. Though he glimpsed the concern in his friends' eyes, they didn't say anything.

Sleep proved elusive once more when he got home. Having spent almost half of his life unconscious, it was if his brain wanted to stay awake. Miles finally fell into a fitful slumber around one a.m.

It was past eight when he woke up. He had a light breakfast and changed into running shorts and a T-shirt. A distant rumble of thunder reached him as he finished tying up his laces and went out on the porch.

Miles eyed the few dark clouds creeping over the mountains while he warmed and stretched his muscles. He'd gotten into the habit of going for a run every morning, about a month after he'd come home. That's how long it had taken for him to lose the walking stick he'd been given to stabilize his gait while his body recovered from its extended period of inactivity.

Miles was grateful for the extensive physiotherapy he'd received while he'd been out cold for twelve years. It meant he hadn't been stuck in a wheelchair when he'd left the care home. Still, he was keen to get back to the level of fitness he'd maintained before the accident.

Of all the Terrible Seven, he'd been the best at track and field when they'd been in high school.

Exercise was also the only way he'd found to soothe his muddled mind.

Something caught Miles's eye when he started down the path that cut across his front yard.

The house opposite had an "Under Contract" board pinned above the "For Sale" sign that had been there the past couple of months.

Miles had been crushed when he'd found out the couple who'd lived there had passed away. He'd really liked the Beattys. According to Elaine, the house had been closed up for some time before the couple's son finally put it on the market the week before Miles had woken up.

I wonder who bought it.

Miles started into a low jog and soon forgot about his mystery new neighbor. The crisp morning air tickled his nostrils, bringing with it the fresh scent of pine and cedar from the nearby forest. He picked up speed and soon lost himself in the rhythm of the physical activity, his breaths coming in steady pants as he pounded the pavement.

It was in these moments that he felt truly alive. His pounding heart. The feel of his warm muscles bunching and relaxing under his powerful strides. The wind in his hair. His mouth curved in a smile at the exhilarating feeling. Even the light rain that started falling couldn't curb his thrill.

The cramp hit him at two miles.

Miles winced and hobbled to a stop. His chest

heaved as he bent over and massaged his treacherous left thigh and calf, a bead of sweat trickling down his temple.

The physiotherapist had warned him he'd still get muscle spasms from time to time.

The rain intensified. He frowned at the sky.

The storm had arrived much faster than he'd anticipated.

It took a couple of minutes for the pangs in his leg to fade. He was about to start jogging again when he heard a faint cry.

Miles tensed, his gaze swinging to the woods lining the footpath on his left. He was in a park on the edge of a residential area. The nearest thoroughfare wasn't busy. What little traffic he'd encountered that morning had already died down.

Bar the pitter-patter of the falling rain and the sound of his own heartbeat, he couldn't hear anything.

Did I imagine it?

A boom shook the heavens, startling him. Lightning flashed far off to his right. Miles eyed the tree tops in the park warily.

I should get out of here.

He turned and had barely taken two steps when something yelped and whimpered in a clump of bushes under a tree, some fifteen feet from his position. Miles stared at the undergrowth, his pulse thrumming in his veins.

The whimper came again.

It sounded like a wounded animal.

Miles hesitated before stepping under the cover of

the trees and heading over to where he'd heard the noise. He carefully parted the thicket.

A pair of sad, soulful blue eyes stared up at him.

They belonged to a black German Shepherd puppy. He looked to be about two months old and sat shivering miserably in a wet cardboard box, briar clinging to his fur.

Miles looked around. Bar an elderly couple seeking shelter in the gazebo by a small lake, it was empty.

The dog whimpered again. Miles's heart twisted.

"Hey there, buddy," he said softly.

The puppy's ears pricked. He stayed still as Miles reached down and picked him up. Alarm clenched Miles's belly when the rain washed away a trace of blood from his fur.

The puppy had a nasty cut on his leg.

Miles cradled him to his chest. "You're going to be okay."

The dog sagged in his arms, as if he'd been waiting a long time to hear those words. He hesitated before stretching his head and carefully licking Miles's chin.

Warmth flooded Miles's chest.

He shielded the dog with his arm and headed out of the park.

CHAPTER THREE

Logan Prescott signed the contract and passed it over to the realtor.

Kelsey Dunn smiled at him across the desk. "Congratulations, Mr. Prescott. I'll get you the keys to your new home next week."

Relief drained some of Logan's tension away.

It finally felt like he could call Twilight Falls his home.

"Please, Logan is fine. Besides, we'll see each other in town at some point."

"Oh, it'll be sooner than that," Kelsey said drily. "I'm bringing my cat for her annual checkup on Monday."

Logan recalled the practice schedule he'd glanced at that morning. "Let me guess, the Siamese?"

Kelsey's mouth fell open. "How did you know?!"

"Her fur's on your jacket," Logan drawled.

Kelsey's head jerked to the coat rack in her office. "Oh."

Logan chuckled at her expression. "Sorry to shatter your illusion. I'm definitely not a mind reader."

Kelsey flushed. She rose to accompany him to the door.

"How are things coming along at the practice?"

Logan could see her interest from the way she stole a glance at him from under her lashes.

"As I expected, to be honest," he replied, keeping his tone mild. "My uncle's been running the place for close to forty years. It'll be a while before people get used to the fact that I'm their new vet."

Curiosity sparked in Kelsey's eyes as they exited the building. "Was it always your intention to move to Twilight Falls when he retired?"

Logan hesitated. He surprised himself a little when he ended up giving her a candid answer.

"Not really." He looked out over the busy Main Street and the enchanting valley rising around the town. Even though it was winter and a light storm was sweeping across the mountains, Twilight Falls looked breathtaking. "But I'm glad I did."

Logan bade the realtor goodbye and jogged across the street to where he'd parked his pickup. His Basset Hound, Pepper, woofed quietly in the front passenger seat when he got in.

Logan closed the door and scratched her under her chin. "Did you miss me, girl?"

She woofed again, her eyes shrinking to blissful slits.

"Wanna grab breakfast at your favorite diner before we go to work?"

Pepper panted and grinned, her tail beating enthusiastically. She plopped down on her belly and rested her head on his thigh as he switched on the ignition and pulled away from the curb.

Logan's gaze swept the colorful forests blanketing the mountains as he drove up Main Street, the wipers swinging steadily across the windshield. The trees were dressed in vivid greens and reds that made the valley live up to its reputation as one of the prettiest places in the San Bernardino Mountains.

Twilight Falls had first seen life as a mining settlement, during the American Gold Rush. It could have ended up like so many other small towns up and down the country, practically deserted but for their historic buildings and with an aging population that would soon die out as the younger people moved to the cities for a better life, leaving behind a lost legacy.

From what his uncle had told him, Twilight Falls had been popular even before he'd first moved there. Successive mayors and a zealous local council had worked hard over the years to make it an attractive place for investors and small businesses, as well as young working couples. The town had only grown from strength to strength since and was now a favorite holiday destination for many of the state's winter sports thrill seekers and those seeking a slower pace of life.

Logan soon pulled up outside a pretty, red brick building with an art deco frontage, a couple of miles from the center of Twilight Falls.

His uncle had recommended the diner when he'd

first moved there. A family run affair that was popular with locals and tourists, it served the best breakfast this side of the San Bernardino Mountains and offered stunning views over the river cutting through the valley. It was also dog friendly in more ways than one.

Logan found an empty spot near a window and ordered a fried breakfast for himself and a doggy breakfast for Pepper. Though the place was busy, their waitress gave the hound an extra egg and topped up Logan's coffee more than once. From the way she stole glances at him when she thought he wasn't looking, Logan guessed she was as curious about him as Kelsey had been.

Logan's eyes glanced off the faint, pale mark on his left ring finger as he took a sip of his coffee. It was the only sign that he'd once been married.

Contrary to most divorces, he and his wife Amanda had parted amicably two years ago. They'd been separated for a year before that.

They'd met when he was at the end of his veterinary residency and had wed after a whirlwind romance. Though Amanda claimed they had never been right for one another from the get-go, Logan blamed himself for their marriage failing.

It wasn't just because his job in Sacramento had been hectic and he'd barely had time for his wife.

Logan had slowly been coming to terms with the fact that he was interested in men.

It had been a vague fascination when he was in high school and college, one he'd thought would pass after he started dating women. It was only when he realized his sex life with Amanda had all but dried up that he finally took a good, hard look at himself and admitted the truth he had long avoided.

Amanda had not been surprised when he'd confessed this to her. They'd remained friends after they'd gone their separate ways and he'd been pleased to hear she was dating again.

Logan finally picked up the courage to go to a gay bar a few months after his divorce was finalized. Considering his looks, it hadn't been difficult for him to find a partner willing to help him explore his sexuality for the night.

Logan soon realized he had more than a healthy sex drive and that his lack of libido had had everything to do with sleeping with the wrong gender for most of his adult life.

Although he'd come out of the closet to his family and closest friends, he was reluctant to share his newfound sexual preference with perfect strangers. Logan was aware Twilight Falls was pretty on board with these things and boasted a hugely popular gay bar. His uncle had even told him about a famous group of local friends who'd openly embraced their homosexuality years ago.

Still, shouting to everyone that he was looking for a casual male sexual partner to share his bed with was hardly going to land Logan in the locals' good books. That kind of thing would be more awkward to do in a small town like Twilight Falls. Though he'd dated a few guys in Sacramento, he wasn't ready for anything serious yet.

Maybe I should check out that gay bar.

The storm intensified when he was driving back to the practice. It took just under fifteen minutes to get there even with the bad weather. Compared to his hourly commute in Sacramento, it was practically heaven.

The parking lot that wrapped around the rambling, two-story clapboard farmhouse was empty. His first client wasn't due until eleven thirty and he'd told his staff to take the morning off. Though the afternoon clinic was fully booked, Logan hoped he'd finish on time so he could start packing his stuff in the apartment above the practice. With most of his things still in a storage unit in town, he didn't have much to put in boxes.

His uncle had offered him his home before he'd left town to go on a golf tour in Mexico. Logan hadn't wanted to impose and had insisted on using the apartment above the practice while he looked for a house to buy.

His uncle had already done more than enough to help him since he'd moved here from Sacramento.

Pepper waited patiently in the rear utility area for Logan to dry her when they came in through the back door. She padded inside the building ahead of him, her claws clicking on the hardwood floor. Logan had just put the coffee machine on when a distant pounding came from the front of the building.

Logan's hands stilled on the towel he'd been using to rub his hair. He glanced at the clock on the wall. It was ten fifteen.

He frowned. It had to be an emergency.

Though the local vets in the area collaborated to run an on-call roster, no one turned away an animal in need.

Logan rolled up his sleeves and headed through a prep area with two operating rooms and an ICU opening off it. The pounding came again, the sound more frantic than before.

Logan walked past the clinic rooms and entered the waiting area. He made out a distorted figure through the frosted glass panel in the top of the front door as he walked around the reception desk.

Pepper was already in the main foyer, her low whines telling him he'd been right on the money.

Logan hoped whatever the animal was, it wasn't in a bad shape.

He unbolted the door and reached for the handle. Lightning flashed and thunder boomed just as he pulled it open. Logan squinted at the bright glare before blinking away the afterglow.

His breath caught.

A man stood on the porch. He was dressed in running shorts and a T-shirt, was soaked to the skin, and was cradling a trembling black German Shepherd puppy in his arms.

Awareness slammed in Logan when he met the stranger's eyes.

Damn. This guy is gorgeous.

The stranger swallowed. "I—I'm sorry." His gaze darted to the closed sign on the wall next to the door. "I saw the notice, but you were the nearest vet I knew of."

Logan looked out into the car park. It was empty.

"You walked here?" he said, incredulous.

The man bit his lip and nodded. Logan's gaze dropped to his mouth.

It was full and lush and ripe enough to bite.

Whoa.

Logan startled at the illicit direction his thoughts had just taken.

The stranger shivered and hugged the puppy. "Can we come in?"

Logan cursed himself and moved aside. "Of course. I apologize, I was just surprised you came here on foot, in this weather." He closed the door and frowned at the man. "We should get you out of those clothes."

The guy did a double take. "Pardon?"

Logan cursed himself for a whole other reason then.

Color was staining the man's ears and cheekbones a delicate pink. He looked like a deer in the headlights. A sexy, skittish, and entirely delectable deer with brown eyes he could drown in.

And Logan was very much starting to feel like a wolf.

CHAPTER FOUR

MILES'S HEART THUDDED AGAINST HIS RIBS AS HE STARED at the attractive, dark-haired man studying him across the foyer. The stranger had a few inches on him and was blessed with the most striking gray-blue eyes Miles had ever seen.

They reminded him of an ocean just before a storm.

"You'll catch a cold if you stay in those," the man said steadily, indicating Miles's wet shorts and T-shirt.

Heat flooded Miles's cheeks. He'd evidently misunderstood the guy.

He swallowed to hide his embarrassment. He'd expected to see the old vet who'd run the practice when he'd come knocking at the door, not some hot guy who probably turned heads wherever he went.

"Is Mr. Prescott here?" Miles said, unable to mask the hope in his voice.

The guy's mouth twitched. "I'm Mr. Prescott. Logan Prescott. I suspect you're looking for my uncle Tom. He's retired. I've just taken over his clinic."

Miles blinked. "Oh. I'm sorry, I didn't know." He paused awkwardly. "I'm Miles. Miles Martinez."

Logan smiled faintly. "It's nice to meet you, Miles."

Miles's pulse quickened.

Logan observed the puppy. "Why don't I take a look at this little guy while you get yourself dry?"

Miles relaxed a little. "I wouldn't mind a towel if you have one."

"I'm staying in the apartment on the second floor, so you might as well get yourself properly dry." Logan's gaze skimmed Miles's body. "I should have some clothes that will fit you."

Miles's belly contracted. He wasn't sure why he was so self-conscious around this guy.

"Are you sure?" he mumbled.

Amusement brightened Logan's eyes. "You're hardly giving me serial killer vibes so, yeah, I'm sure."

Miles flushed. "Alright."

He almost winced at the breathy way the word came out.

God, he must think I'm a fool.

Miles stiffened slightly when Logan took the puppy from him. He felt reluctant to let go of the dog for some reason.

"I found him in a box, by the side of the road."

Logan raised an eyebrow. "He isn't yours?" He examined the cut on the puppy's leg, his touch gentle.

"No. I'm not sure how long he was out there."

The puppy whimpered, ears and tail drooping. He stared sorrowfully at Miles from the vet's arms, his miserable gaze accusing him of abandoning him. Miles's heart twisted.

A low woof had both he and the puppy freezing.

Miles looked down. He hadn't noticed the Basset Hound sitting quietly by Logan.

"Her name's Pepper," Logan said without looking up. He finished inspecting the injured puppy's leg and scratched him between the ears. The dog closed his eyes and slowly wagged his tail. "This cut should heal fine once it's cleaned and glued." His mouth curved when he met Miles's gaze. "He's in pretty good shape otherwise. He's lucky you found him. I suspect whoever abandoned him did it this morning."

Miles's stomach flip-flopped again at Logan's smile.

"That's—that's great," he practically squeaked.

Miles swallowed a groan.

What is wrong with me?!

If Logan noticed his nervousness, he didn't say anything. He guided Miles inside the practice and led him to a staircase at the back of the building.

"The apartment's at the top, on the left. It's pretty small so you shouldn't have any trouble finding anything." Logan fished a key out of his jeans and dropped it in Miles's hand. "Towels are in the bathroom. You'll find T-shirts and jogging bottoms in the dresser."

Miles curled his fingers over the metal. It was warm from Logan's body heat.

"I feel like I'm imposing," he said, contrite.

"And I'm pretty sure you'll catch a cold if you stay in those clothes," Logan countered adamantly. "So how about you save me the guilt trip and go change into something dry?"

"Okay," Miles murmured. "Thanks."

He took the stairs, conscious of Logan's gaze on his back.

The apartment was warm and cozy. Miles's gaze skimmed the double bed on the other side of the living area.

It felt strangely intimate being in another man's bedroom.

Or anyone's bedroom for that matter.

He headed into the bathroom, his chest tight and his face warm.

Miles looked longingly at the shower before kicking off his socks and shoes and reaching for the bottom of his T-shirt. He was shrugging it off his shoulders when a knock came at the bathroom door. Miles startled.

He'd left it ajar.

"Er, come in."

The door swung open.

"I forgot to say, feel free to have a shower if you—" Logan stilled, one foot inside the room. His eyes widened at the sight of Miles. A strange expression flitted across his face. "I'm sorry, I didn't mean to walk in on you. I was just going to say you should warm yourself up with a hot shower before you get into dry clothes."

Miles clutched his T-shirt to his chest, his pulse racing and his mouth inexplicably dry. "Thank you. I—

I'll take you up on that offer." His tongue darted out to lick his lower lip.

Logan's gaze locked on his mouth.

Miles held his breath when the air between them sparked.

Logan clenched his jaw and dipped his head curtly before disappearing, his posture strangely stiff.

Miles waited until he heard the apartment door close before releasing the breath he'd been holding.

What was that about?!

He wondered if he'd upset Logan.

Miles's stomach knotted as he stripped distractedly out of his shorts and boxers and got under the shower.

I did turn up at his clinic unannounced.

He almost groaned when the hot water hit his skin.

He hadn't realized how cold he'd been.

Miles eyed Logan's shampoo and body wash. He hesitated before reaching for them.

The lather was silky and smelled of mint and cedar.

His body tingled all over as he rubbed it into his skin and hair.

This feels even more intimate than being in Logan's bedroom.

A shiver of arousal raced through his cock.

Miles blinked, shocked. He looked down before lowering his hand. A pleasurable sensation shot through him as his sensitized shaft responded to his touch. He flushed.

I can't believe I'm getting hard in another man's shower!

Miles took a shaky breath and counted sheep while

he hastily rinsed his hair and the soap suds clinging to his skin.

To his relief, his burgeoning erection had settled by the time he took a bath sheet from the pile on a shelf and dried himself. He wrapped the towel around his body, wrung out his wet clothes in the sink, and put them in a garbage bag he found under the sink.

Miles ventured out in Logan's bedroom and headed for the dresser, the floorboards cool under his bare feet. He opened the top drawer and froze.

It contained Logan's underwear and socks.

A purple box peeked out from beneath some boxers.

Miles's heartbeat sounded loud in his ears as he stared at the pack of condoms.

He shut the drawer hastily and crunched his eyes closed, his breaths coming hard and fast like he'd just run a marathon. His sex throbbed mockingly between his thighs.

He didn't even have to look to know he was growing erect again.

Maybe I'm coming down with something. Miles swallowed convulsively. *That's the only possible reason as to why I'm acting like a horny teen in a stranger's bedroom right now.*

He rooted through the other drawers, found a T-shirt and jogging bottoms he thought would fit him, and dressed hastily, his face so hot he was surprised he hadn't self-combusted.

Pepper was sitting on the landing when he came out of the apartment with the bag holding his clothes and trainers.

The dog woofed softly, rose, and headed down the stairs. She stopped halfway and looked at him expectantly. Miles followed her.

Logan's voice reached him when they neared the prep room.

"Who's a good boy?"

The puppy yipped, a happy sound.

Miles slowed as he came in sight of the pair.

The puppy was lying on his belly on an examination table. He gnawed at a chew toy while Logan bandaged his leg.

Miles couldn't help but stare at the vet's powerful forearms and his large, strong hands as he finished wrapping the dressing. His belly tightened all over again.

"Hey." Logan brightened when he saw him. "I'm pretty much done here. Want a coffee?"

Miles nodded, tongue-tied.

CHAPTER FIVE

Logan's pulse thrummed as he rose from the stool.

Thank God my dick calmed down.

Seeing Miles half-naked in his bathroom had done things to his libido Logan hadn't experienced in a while. He'd been rock hard by the time he'd emerged on the landing outside the apartment. Much to his embarrassment, he'd had to think of complex chemical formulas to bring his raging erection under control.

His stomach clenched with desire when he caught a whiff of his shampoo and body wash wafting off Miles. To say that he was stunned by the insta-lust he was feeling toward a guy he'd just met would be putting things mildly.

Logan couldn't remember being this captivated by another person, be they female or male.

The puppy made a worried sound as he came around the table.

"It's okay, boy." Logan ruffled his head. "Pepper will

keep you company." He lifted the dog and placed him in a basket on the floor.

Pepper climbed in and curled her body around the puppy before he could attempt to get out. The puppy faltered before settling down beside her.

"He doesn't have a microchip, so he's definitely been abandoned," Logan said thoughtfully. He smiled when the puppy carefully licked Pepper's face. "That should keep him happy for a while." He turned to Miles. "Shall we?"

Miles nodded and followed Logan to the kitchen.

Logan's skin prickled with awareness as he made them coffee. The room wasn't exactly small. Yet he couldn't help but be conscious of Miles's every breath and move.

Miles looked around curiously. "Did you close for the whole day?"

"Only the morning." Logan handed him a steaming cup. "I had an appointment I couldn't miss."

Miles blew on his coffee before taking a sip.

Logan leaned a hip against the counter. "So, how come you walked here?"

"I was out for a run." Miles shrugged. "I only live a few miles from here."

"Are you off work today?" Logan asked before he could help himself.

Miles's expression grew strained.

Logan winced. "I'm sorry. I didn't mean to pry."

"You aren't," Miles said quietly. "I'm…not working right now."

He ducked his head and drank his coffee.

Logan stared. *Curiouser and curiouser.*

Miles's clothes and trainers looked expensive.

"Oh." Logan straightened. "I should put your stuff in the dryer."

"It's okay, I can take the clothes home," Miles protested. "Besides, I need to wash these and bring them back." He tugged at the T-shirt he was wearing.

Logan was about to object when he realized this would give him another opportunity to see Miles. "Okay."

He'd just placed Miles's trainers in one of the dryers in the utility area when the back door opened.

"Whoa, this storm is something else!" A redhead with her hair in a ponytail came in, shook out her umbrella, and shrugged out of her raincoat. She was wearing a dark blue veterinary nurse uniform beneath it and had a badge with her name pinned to her chest.

Logan swallowed a curse. "I wasn't expecting you until later."

Lucy Whitlock was the biggest gossip in the practice and quite likely the entire town. In the month since he'd officially taken over his uncle's clinic, Logan had learned more than he needed to know about the private lives of his employees, as well as those of several people of interest in Twilight Falls.

"I had some paperwork to take care of." Lucy arched an eyebrow. "Besides, your eleven thirty appointment is Lola. She's the biggest Neapolitan Mastiff this side of the San Bernardino Mountains. The last time she came in for a check-up, three of us practically had to sit on her."

Logan's mouth pressed to a thin line. "I'm sure I can convince Lola to co-operate."

Lucy made a face. "Look, I'm not gonna deny that you're a tall glass of awesomeness, but Lola is a dog, not a human. You can't charm the pants off her."

"Ha-ha," Logan grumbled.

"What's got you so antsy?" Lucy said, puzzled.

A yip came from the direction of the prep room.

"Oh." Her gaze shifted to the hallway. "You got company?"

Logan sighed. There was no avoiding the inevitable. "Yeah."

Lucy trailed in his steps as he exited the utility area.

Miles had come out of the kitchen and was keeping the dogs company.

Lucy stared. Curiosity burned brightly on her face as she glanced at Logan.

Logan reluctantly made the introductions.

"Miles, this is Lucy Whitlock, the senior nurse at the clinic. She's also my practice manager. Lucy, this is Miles Martinez."

Lucy's eyes rounded. She sucked in air and pressed her hands to her mouth. "You're one of the Terrible Seven!"

Miles looked like he wanted to sink into the ground.

Logan lowered his brows at his practice manager.

Lucy's expression turned sheepish. "I'm sorry," she told Miles apologetically. "I couldn't help it. You guys are practically royalty in this town."

"It's alright." Miles grimaced and rubbed the back of

his neck. "Don't let Hunter hear you say that. It will only inflate his already swollen ego."

Lucy grinned. "I hear Twilight Falls' notorious bad boy has been thoroughly tamed by his fiancé."

"It's more like Hunter is a grouchy lion and Theo is a circus ringmaster," Miles grunted. "How he managed to domesticate that beast is beyond me."

Lucy burst out laughing.

Logan shot an intrigued look at Miles from under his lashes. His uncle hadn't been the only one who'd mentioned the Terrible Seven. Lucy had delighted in telling him tales of Twilight Falls' most famous locals and their better halves, among them a movie star, an internationally renowned artist, a Michelin-star pastry chef, and a rockstar. According to Lucy, they were all hot as hell and made men and women swoon wherever they went.

From Miles's reaction, he didn't like being labeled with the same brush.

Lucy eyed the puppy playing with Pepper. "Is he yours?"

Miles hesitated. "I found him on the side of the road this morning."

Lucy's face fell. "Oh. That's a shame. He'll have to go to the shelter." She chewed her lip. "I'll make some posters and see if anyone wants to adopt him."

Miles flinched. "No!"

Logan and Lucy stared.

Miles flushed. "I'm sorry. I—I would like to keep him if that's okay." He squatted by the basket and picked up the puppy.

A faint frown wrinkled Logan's brow as Miles hugged the puppy defensively to his chest. "Have you ever owned a dog?"

"Yes." Miles lowered his gaze, his tone strained. "He passed away shortly before I became…ill."

Logan's stomach twisted. *Wait. Is he sick?*

He was about to ask Miles if he was okay when he caught Lucy's warning look.

"In that case, why don't I get some paperwork ready so we can register him and book him in for his vaccinations?" the practice manager said warmly. "Do you know what you're going to call him?"

Miles straightened. "Oh," he mumbled. "I hadn't thought about that."

His crestfallen expression had Logan biting back a smile.

He realized he liked watching Miles's face change with his emotions.

It makes me want to find out what he'll look like during sex.

That thought sent a shiver down Logan's spine and made his belly knot.

Shit. This guy really does push all my buttons in the right way.

By the time Lucy finished registering the puppy, Miles's trainers had dried and the storm had all but passed. Logan was about to suggest he drop Miles home when Lola the mastiff arrived with her owner.

"It's okay," Miles protested when Lucy offered to take him instead. "Honestly, my house isn't far."

Logan reluctantly saw Miles to the door, surprised by what he was feeling.

He'd wanted to spend more time with him.

A couple of cars pulled into the parking lot as Miles stepped out onto the porch. The practice staff were arriving ahead of the afternoon clinic.

Pepper woofed, a sad sound.

Miles stooped and scratched the hound's head. "Thanks for looking after him, Pepper."

Pepper propped her forepaws on his knees and licked his face. The puppy joined in. Miles chuckled.

The sound shot straight to Logan's gut.

He forced himself to smile and offered Miles his hand. "See you soon."

Miles rose and shook his hand.

Electricity sparked between their skin.

The hairs rose on Logan's nape.

Miles's breath caught, his lips parting and his pupils dilating with the same heightened awareness heating up Logan's blood. He snatched his hand away.

"Thanks for everything," he said in a flustered voice. He turned and practically ran down the steps.

Logan watched him leave, his heart racing. The look on Miles's face had been unmistakable.

He was attracted to Logan too.

CHAPTER SIX

MILES THREW THE BALL ACROSS THE BACKYARD. THE
puppy yipped and bolted through the freshly cut grass.
He snatched the toy where it'd landed and returned to
Miles, ears flopping and tail swinging so fast it
practically blurred.

"Good boy, Blue." Miles squatted and scratched the
puppy under the chin when he dropped the ball at his
feet.

Blue made a happy sound. He dropped down onto
the grass, his tongue lolling as he panted.

Miles gave him his bowl of water and sat
beside him.

He raised his face to the blazing sun and the clear,
blue sky.

It was Saturday morning. The last of the storm that
had swept through the valley a week ago had finally
cleared. Not that Miles had taken much notice of the
weather. He'd been too busy buying things for Blue at

the pet stores Lucy had recommended and house training the puppy.

Miles had told Wyatt and Izzy about the dog yesterday. They were planning to drop by in the afternoon to meet Blue.

Knowing Izzy, I wouldn't be surprised if the whole gang turns up.

His chest tightened as he thought of Logan. The vet had been in surgery when he'd gone to the practice on Monday to drop off the clothes he'd borrowed from him. Lucy had come out to greet Miles instead and promised to pass on his thanks.

Miles drew his legs up and rested his folded arms atop his knees, the disappointment he'd felt at the time echoing keenly through him.

He hadn't been able to stop thinking about Logan.

I want to see him again.

It was strange how much he missed the man considering he didn't even know he existed a week ago.

Miles's stomach knotted. He couldn't deny that he found Logan attractive. But it wasn't just Logan's looks that had captured his interest.

There was a quiet strength and confidence to Logan that Miles really liked.

Blue yipped and jumped on him. Miles laughed as the puppy tried to tackle him to the ground. He played with him for a while longer and was about to go in and start on lunch when the low rumble of an engine came from the road.

Blue's ears pricked up. Miles stilled.

It's too early for Wyatt and Izzy to be here.

His house was around a bend, at the end of a cul-de-sac that gave way to woodland. The only property close by was the Beattys' old place.

A door slammed somewhere out front.

A man's faint voice reached him.

Miles frowned faintly. He climbed to his feet with Blue in his arms and walked around the side of the house, curious as to the source of the commotion.

A pickup with a removal trailer was parked in front of the Beattys' old home. Miles stared.

The new neighbor must be here.

A familiar woof had him pulling up short.

Miles's gaze swung to the truck. His eyes widened.

Blue yipped and wriggled excitedly in his hold.

Pepper sat in the passenger seat of the vehicle. She propped her paws on the edge of the open window and woofed again, head bobbing and tail wagging.

"Miles?"

Miles's shocked gaze swiveled to the startled man who'd just appeared from behind the trailer. His pulse spiked.

"Lo—Logan?!" he stammered.

"You live here?" Logan's surprised gaze moved past Miles.

"Yes." Miles's pulse fluttered as he crossed his front yard and headed across the road.

"Well, I'll be damned." Logan smiled wryly. "I never thought in a million years we'd end up being neighbors."

Miles swallowed. "You bought the Beattys' place?"

"Yeah." Logan turned to look at the property. "It came on the market at the perfect time. My realtor warned me it would get snatched up fast so I made certain to put in an offer on the day it went up for sale."

A thrill coursed through Miles. He couldn't believe Logan was going to live opposite him. He glanced at the trailer.

"Do you need a hand?"

Logan hesitated. "I wouldn't mind some help, but only if you don't have other plans."

"I don't. My plans today consisted of playing with Blue and entertaining some friends."

Logan's mouth curved in a grin that made Miles's breath catch. "So you finally gave him a name, huh?"

"Yes." Miles ducked his head, his cheeks warming.

Logan came over and scratched Blue's head. "You can leave him with Pepper. She'll make sure he doesn't wander far."

Miles's skin prickled at Logan's closeness and his body heat.

Logan let Pepper out of the pickup and guided her into their new backyard. Blue whined excitedly when Miles put him down next to the hound. The dogs ran playfully through the grass.

Logan and Miles walked back around to the front.

"Is that all you have?" Miles indicated the trailer.

"Yeah." Logan undid the lock on the doors and pulled them open. "It's mostly boxes. I only brought a few pieces of furniture with me when I moved here from Sacramento." He smiled wryly. "I wanted to make a fresh start."

Miles looked curiously at Logan as he grabbed a carton. "Did you sell the rest of your things?"

"Not quite," Logan replied lightly. "My ex-wife bought me out and kept most of our furniture. I rented a place after we got divorced."

"Oh." A sinking feeling formed in the pit of Miles's stomach.

Logan took a box and led the way up the porch, oblivious to his dismay.

Miles was glad Logan couldn't see his face as he followed.

He'd wondered if the sizzle of attraction he'd felt between them the day they'd met had been a fluke. Now that he knew Logan used to be married to a woman, there was no point asking himself that question anymore.

He's obviously not into guys.

Miles took a shallow breath and headed into the house after Logan, determined not to let his chagrin show. The interior was cleaner than he'd thought it would be.

"I hired a company to spruce up the place," Logan explained as his surprised expression. "Just leave the boxes in the dining room. I'll go through them afterward."

It was early afternoon by the time they finished unloading the trailer. Perspiration beaded Miles's forehead where he sat on the porch step. They'd just finished moving the sofa bed Logan had brought into the living room.

It felt good to be physically active.

Miles realized he'd been at risk of spending yet another weekend idling his time away.

I need to decide what I want to do with my life.

Though the psychologist he'd been seeing since he'd woken up from his coma had warned him he shouldn't make any life changing decisions until next year, Miles knew sitting at home doing nothing was going to drive him crazy. And he would fall even further behind his friends.

He thought of the college brochures he'd ordered a couple of weeks ago. The ones currently sitting in unopened envelopes in his bedside drawer.

Seeing how hard Logan had worked to move to another town to start a new life was the final push he needed to get over his crippling indecisiveness.

Logan came out of the house, oblivious to the thoughts swirling through Miles's mind and his fresh conviction. "I think all that hard work deserves a beer."

Miles put away his concerns and arched an eyebrow. "You have beer?"

Logan grinned. He went over to his pickup and returned with a cooler.

Miles smiled when the vet handed him a chilled bottle. "You came prepared."

"Well, I thought I'd deserve a reward if I was going to be at this all afternoon." Logan's expression turned teasing. "Luckily, my handsome new neighbor decided to help me out."

Miles's ears grew warm. He looked away, not sure what to make of the compliment.

"I think this beer will go well with a pastrami sandwich."

Logan looked impressed. "You have pastrami sandwiches?"

Miles laughed. "I was going to make lunch for me and Blue. Why don't you and Pepper come over?"

Logan's face softened. "I won't say no to that."

MILES'S BELLY FLIP-FLOPPED. HE ROSE TO HIS FEET AND swallowed.

Dammit. I need to come to my senses. Logan isn't interested in me.

Logan locked up and fetched the dogs before following Miles across the road. Miles couldn't help feel self-conscious when Logan entered the hallway of his home.

"Do you live here alone?" Logan asked quizzically.

"No." Miles headed for the kitchen. "My mom's on a cruise. It's her first holiday in…well, in a while."

He wondered if Lucy had told Logan about his circumstances. Considering how much she seemed to know about the Terrible Seven, there was a good chance she'd mentioned the accident and his coma.

Miles removed the container of fresh rice, chicken, and vegetables he'd made for Blue the night before from the refrigerator and warmed it up in the microwave.

"That's way fancier than the food Pepper gets most days," Logan drawled.

Pepper woofed in agreement. She plopped her bottom down next to Blue and his feeding station. Miles got a second bowl out for the hound while Logan topped up the dogs' water.

Logan leaned against the counter and sipped his beer as he watched Miles prepare their sandwiches.

"Lucy said you'd dropped by. Thanks for bringing the clothes back."

"It was the least I could do," Miles murmured.

Though his heartbeat sounded loud in his ears, he did his best to appear composed. Considering Logan's gaze felt like it was scorching him, he thought he was doing a pretty good job.

Miles plated their food and took it over to the table. Logan followed with their beers.

The vet groaned when he took his first bite of the sandwich. "Oh my God. What is this?" He chewed with healthy enthusiasm.

Miles smiled. "It's the sauce."

Logan swallowed and looked at him blankly. "You made it yourself?"

Miles chuckled at his awed tone. "I wish I could take the credit, but no. Elijah gave me the recipe." He paused. "He's a friend of mine. He owns—"

"*La Petite Bouche Gourmande.*" A dry smile twisted Logan's mouth. "Lucy waxed lyrical about the man. Between his cakes and his movie star husband, I'm pretty sure Lucy would choose his cakes." He took another bit of the sandwich and groaned again. "Man, if this guy's baked goods is anywhere as good as this sauce, I can see why people line up to get into his place."

A soft smile tugged at Miles's lips. He and Elijah had become fast friends. It was probably because their personalities were so alike.

Miles finished his sandwich and drank half his beer before finally getting up the courage to ask Logan the question he'd been afraid to voice.

"Did Lucy tell you anything about me?"

⁂

LOGAN WASN'T FOOLED BY MILES'S STEADY TONE.

Miles's knuckles were white where he clasped his beer bottle.

"She mentioned an accident," Logan said lightly.

Considering his practice manager routinely blabbed about virtually anyone who crossed Logan's path, Lucy had been surprisingly reticent to tell him more about Miles. Bar clarifying that the illness Miles had mentioned the day he'd visited the practice had actually been an accident, she'd kept mum on the subject.

Miles lowered his gaze and toyed with his bottle.

A strained silence followed. Miles finally spoke.

"We were eighteen when it happened. It was July Fourth. We were going to our favorite picnic spot to watch the fireworks. We…never made it there."

Logan's heart twisted at Miles's bereft look.

Blue lifted his head and whined softly where he'd

settled in his basket with Pepper, as if he could sense the grief and bitterness Miles was trying to mask. Logan suspected the dog probably could.

Animals were a lot more attuned to human emotions than humans themselves were.

Miles startled when Logan reached over and put his hand on top of his fist.

"It's okay," Logan said quietly. "We don't have to talk about this if you don't want to."

Miles's skin heated up Logan's flesh, just like it had done that day at the clinic. Except this time, he hoped his touch would bring Miles solace instead of making him nervous.

Miles took a shaky breath and met Logan's concerned stare. "I want to, actually." He almost looked surprised at his own words.

Logan kept his hand atop Miles's as he started talking again.

"Alex was driving his mom's pickup that day. All seven of us were there." A melancholic light dawned in Miles's eyes. "We'd been inseparable since middle school."

Logan's pulse quickened. "What happened?"

"A drunk driver came down the mountain on the wrong side of the road. If it hadn't been for Alex's reflexes, we would have gone off a cliff. He turned the steering wheel toward the forest and we smashed into a tree instead." Miles's expression turned haunted. "The last thing I remember is the headlights of that other guy's car. Of the seven of us, six walked out of that accident pretty much unscathed. I didn't."

Logan's stomach hardened. He could see how much the memory of that day still affected Miles.

"Have you spoken to someone? I mean, a professional?" he said, troubled. "It sounds like you still have a lot to process even after all these years."

Miles blinked at his words. "Oh. I only woke up two months ago."

Logan stared, not sure he'd heard right. "What?"

Miles's shoulders knotted. He pulled his hand away, his voice turning brittle. "I mean, I was in a coma. For twelve years."

His words reverberated around the kitchen.

Logan's head spun. *He was in a coma?!*

Miles's face grew shuttered at Logan's shocked expression. "I'm sorry, I shouldn't have brought this—"

"Don't." Logan shook his head before taking Miles's hand again, cursing himself for his reaction. "I'm sorry. I just…wasn't expecting you to say that." He squeezed Miles's fingers, his heart aching at everything he had gone through. Though he didn't know the full details of what had happened in the aftermath of the accident, he could guess how harrowing it must have been for all those involved. Even more so for the man who sat across from him with an agonizing look in his dark eyes. "How are you doing?" Logan said after a pause. "I mean, *really* doing?"

Miles's face tightened.

For a moment, Logan feared he would stay in the shell he'd just retreated into. Relief loosened his muscles when Miles spoke.

"Physically, I think I'm okay. Mentally?" A self-deprecating chuckle left Miles. He winced at the sound. "Mentally, I'm a mess." His voice trembled. "I've slept through a third of my life. And now I'm awake again. But…everything is different."

Miles met Logan's gaze, his own so full of despair it rooted Logan's legs to the ground.

"My mom," Miles mumbled. "My friends. This world." He looked blindly out the window before staring at his fingers as if they belonged to someone else. "Even my body feels strange to me. I—I don't know what to do!" His breath hitched. "Oh." Tears bloomed in his eyes. Miles blinked before wiping them hastily with the back of a hand, his face flushing. "I'm sorry, I'm not usually like—!"

Logan finally unfroze. He leaned over and hugged Miles.

Miles stiffened.

Logan could feel Miles's heart thundering against his ribs as he held him.

"You're incredible, Miles," he said quietly. "I don't know much about coma patients, but I bet most of them wouldn't even leave their house at this stage. It's clear as day you're trying everything you can to make your life normal again. You'll be okay, Miles. I'm sure of it." He squeezed his arms around Miles, hoping to convey the wealth of feelings crowding his chest.

Miles shuddered. He clung to Logan, the wetness of his tears soaking into Logan's shoulder.

Blue jumped out of his basket and came over. The puppy propped his forepaws on Miles's leg and whined.

Miles inhaled shakily and chuckled. "I'm alright, Blue."

A keen sense of loss pierced Logan when Miles pulled away from him and bent to ruffle the dog's ears. Blue watched Miles worriedly for a moment before returning to his basket.

"That dog already loves you," Logan said.

Miles sniffed and wiped his cheeks with a napkin. "You think?"

Logan could tell from the way Miles was refusing to meet his eyes that he was embarrassed by what had just happened.

"I'm pretty sure."

Something in his voice had Miles looking up.

Miles's breath caught. His pupils dilated and his lips parted, just like they had done that day at the clinic.

This time, Logan made no attempt to hide what he was feeling for him.

Miles's pulse beat frantically at the base of his throat when Logan gently cradled his chin with his fingers and slowly leaned in.

"Tell me if you don't want this," Logan whispered.

Miles blinked and kept still. His gaze dropped to Logan's mouth.

It was all the invitation Logan needed.

He brushed his lips across Miles's. Miles drew a shaky breath.

Logan repeated the movement. Miles's lashes slowly fluttered closed.

CHAPTER EIGHT

LOGAN'S COCK STIRRED. HE CLASPED MILES'S FACE WITH both hands and angled his head so he could meld their mouths together. Miles grasped his shoulders, his movements jerky. The way his fingers twitched on Logan's flesh and the soft sound working its way up his throat as he held on to Logan told him he liked what he was doing.

Miles's lips were every bit as soft and as sweet as Logan had thought they would be. He groaned and slipped his tongue inside Miles's mouth, eager to savor more of his intoxicating taste.

Miles froze. He pulled away with a gasp, his chest heaving with his breaths.

"I—I thought you weren't into guys!" he said accusingly.

It took all of Logan's willpower not to claim Miles's mouth again. He had a raging erection and he very much wanted to do something about it with the man staring at him with his lips swollen from his kiss and the sexiest frown he'd ever seen.

"I never said that."

"But—but you were married," Miles protested. He glanced at the pale band of skin on Logan's ring finger.

"I got divorced after I came to terms with the fact that I was gay."

Miles's eyes rounded at his blunt admission. "You are?!" he squeaked.

Logan swallowed a chuckle.

Miles all flustered was incredibly endearing. It made Logan want to do all kinds of naughty things to him.

"Yes, I am." Logan raised a hand and ghosted his thumb across Miles's lower lip. "I take it from the way you responded to my kiss that you are too?"

Miles's cheeks brightened with color. "I—" He stopped and swallowed convulsively. "Yes."

Logan cursed internally as Miles's warm breath tickled his flesh.

"Good." He rose, pulled Miles to his feet, and took his mouth in a passionate kiss.

Miles stiffened for an instant. Then he sighed, closed his eyes, and melted into Logan's hold.

Logan groaned and delved inside Miles's mouth, hungry for more. Miles made a surprised sound when Logan fused their tongues together.

A singular truth tore through Logan as Miles kissed him back hesitantly, shocking him to the core. He savored Miles's sweetness and the clumsy movements of his tongue for a moment longer before reluctantly pulling away.

Logan held Miles's hot cheeks and stared into his bright, dazed eyes, his own heart hammering against his ribs.

"Have you ever done this before?"

Miles blinked, awareness slowly returning to his face. The delicate flush that crept across his skin and the way he lowered his gaze was all the answer Logan needed.

"Is that a bad thing?" Miles murmured, his tone defiant despite the quiver in his voice. He looked up at Logan from under his lashes.

Logan bit back a curse. "The fact that you've never had sex? It's such a massive turn on it's a miracle I haven't dragged you upstairs to your bedroom to show you exactly what you've been missing."

Miles drew a sharp breath. Logan couldn't help but laugh at his shocked and equally thrilled expression.

Miles bit his lip. "That was my first kiss too."

Logan's stomach flip-flopped. *Oh, dear God.*

"It was?" he managed to say.

"Yeah." Miles made a face. "Well, technically, that was the second one since you kissed me a minute—" He gasped when Logan took his mouth again.

By the time they came up for air, Miles was panting and Logan was rock hard. Logan pressed his forehead against Miles's brow.

"You're gonna give me a heart attack," he groaned.

Miles's breath caught when Logan's erection probed his thigh.

Logan lowered his hand and stroked the stiff bulge denting the front of Miles's jeans with the back of his knuckles. "So, no one has ever touched you here?"

Miles made a strangled sound. "N—no!"

His cock twitched under Logan's hand.

Logan couldn't have stopped teasing Miles if his life depended on it. His mouth curved in a seductive smile as he trailed his fingers up Miles's trembling belly and across his chest. He found Miles's left nipple through his T-shirt and rubbed it lightly with the pad of his thumb.

"How about here?"

Miles gasped and arched into his touch, his pupils blowing with pleasure. "No one has touched me. Anywhere!"

Logan's heart raced as he looked at the aroused man in his arms.

I can't believe he's a virgin. He's going to make me lose my goddamn mind.

Logan knew he needed to take things slow, but his dick was doing press-ups behind his zipper and he was pretty certain he was going to embarrass himself soon if his body didn't find some kind of release.

The sound of an engine outside the house doused his ardor as effectively as a bucket of cold water. It was followed by several other vehicles.

Miles froze when doors slammed on his driveway. He pressed his lips together. "Those guys have shitty timing."

Logan chuckled at his annoyed moue. "Are those the friends you were expecting?"

"Yeah." Miles sighed. "By the sounds, the whole gang's here."

Footsteps and voices came from the porch. The bell rang.

Logan reluctantly let Miles go. "I'll get the door."

Miles gave him a puzzled look.

"You should probably do something about that before you meet your friends," Logan drawled.

Miles flushed when Logan indicated his erection. He bolted out of the kitchen, his face bright red.

Logan grinned and headed into the foyer.

His pulse quickened a little as he reached for the latch on the door.

He was about to meet Miles's friends. And he realized he very much wanted to make a good first impression.

Christ, I feel like I'm going to greet my future-in-laws.

That startling thought brought Logan up short.

It should have scared him. Except it didn't.

Logan's shoulders unknotted. He couldn't help but sense that things would work out okay, somehow.

He opened the door to a bevy of hot men and a pretty brunette.

They stared at him blankly from across the threshold.

Logan suppressed a wry grin.

I can see why these guys pack a punch wherever they go.

It wasn't just that the men studying him were handsome as sin. They each had an individual presence that would make them stand out in any crowd.

Logan was starting to realize why the Terrible

Seven were universally adored by the folks in Twilight Falls despite having been little terrors in their youths.

"Who are you?" the brunette said, shocked.

She must be Izzy Batista.

Logan smiled. "I'm Logan Prescott, Miles's new neighbor."

Izzy and the men turned to look at the house opposite the road.

"You are?" The guy who'd spoken had an imposing stature, a stubbled jawline, and tattoos running up the side of his neck. He looked warily at Logan.

And that must be Tristan Hart.

For once, Logan was grateful to Lucy. He could practically tell who was who among Miles's famous friends.

"Miles told me he was expecting you." Logan stepped back. "Come on in."

They glanced at each other before crowding inside the foyer and taking off their coats like they'd done this a million times before.

"Looks like you just moved in," a man with green eyes the same shade as the brunette's said in a level tone. He indicated the trailer parked at the curb.

He's gotta be Wyatt Batista, Izzy's brother.

"I did," Logan said. "Miles gave me a hand."

He met the stare of a guy with piercing gray eyes and an intensely curious expression.

"It's not like Miles to invite perfect strangers into his home," the man who Logan suspected was Hunter Thomson drawled.

"Where is Miles by the way?" an attractive blond with pale blue eyes said guardedly.

And that's Alex Hancock-West, the lawyer.

"I'm the vet who took care of Blue when Miles found him," Logan told Hunter mildly. "And Miles is upstairs," he said to Alex.

"Blue?" a ruggedly handsome guy with overlong brown hair grunted.

Logan studied Drake Jackson placidly.

I'm not quite sure who's gunning for my head more, him or the lawyer.

It was clear Miles's friends were incredibly protective of him. Another truth echoed inside Logan then.

It's not that surprising. It must have been frustrating watching Miles in a coma all these years and not being able to help him.

The subject of his thoughts came down the stairs.

Miles looked more composed than he'd been when he'd left the kitchen. From his slightly damp bangs, Logan gathered he'd splashed a lot of water on his face.

Desire knotted his belly despite the curious men and woman next to him. He knew it would only take him a minute to make Miles hot and bothered again.

Miles gave his friends a stern look, oblivious to Logan's filthy thoughts. "What's with the twenty questions? I could hear you guys from upstairs."

"He could have been a serial killer for all we know," Drake said sullenly.

"A serial killer wouldn't open the door," Hunter pointed out.

Drake frowned at Hunter. Tristan sighed. Izzy rolled her eyes.

Blue poked his head out of the kitchen.

Izzy's expression melted when she spotted the puppy. "Oh my God, he's adorable!"

Blue made a worried sound and darted behind Miles's legs.

Izzy's face fell. Hunter swallowed a snort.

"It's okay, Blue," Miles said. "She's not as scary as she looks."

"You're hurting my feelings," Izzy protested.

Miles's friends squatted and tried not to frighten Blue as they said hello to the puppy. Blue sniffed their hands curiously, his tail slowly wagging.

Pepper trotted out of the kitchen and joined Logan.

"We should take our leave," Logan told Miles with a reluctant smile. "I hope you have a fun afternoon."

The expression in Miles's eyes told Logan he was loathed to see him go too.

Logan's gaze glanced off Miles's running shoes where they sat by the door. He stopped, his hand on the door handle.

"Fancy a run tomorrow?"

Miles blinked, surprised. "You run?"

"To be honest, I haven't exercised since I came here." Logan grimaced. "I should get back into it before I get a paunch." He patted his stomach.

Miles's expression softened. "Sure."

CHAPTER NINE

The doorbell rang at eight thirty the next morning. Miles came out of the kitchen and did his best to hide his nerves as he crossed the foyer.

He'd found himself looking out of his living room window at the house opposite the road far too often after his friends had left yesterday. And he hadn't gotten much sleep last night either. For once, it wasn't because his mind was full of tumultuous thoughts about the past.

Instead, Miles had found himself reliving the wicked way Logan had kissed and touched him, to the point he'd ended up stroking himself to a mind-blowing orgasm before he'd fallen asleep.

Miles couldn't help the sliver of doubt that clouded his mind as he reached for the doorknob. His belly clenched.

He and Logan hadn't made any promises yesterday.

Sure, they'd kissed, but Logan hadn't said anything beyond that.

Then again, Izzy and the others turned up before we could talk about what happened between us.

Miles pulled the door open, his insecurities clogging his throat.

Logan turned where he'd been looking out at the mountains. He was wearing running shorts and a T-shirt that showcased his powerful arms and strong legs. His face lit up at the sight of Miles.

"Good morning. You ready?"

Pepper let out a friendly woof by Logan's feet.

Miles's chest loosened. All it took was one look at Logan's beautiful eyes to allay his fears.

He's not the kind of person who'll lead me on or deliberately hurt me.

Miles wasn't sure how he knew this. He just…did. The tension oozed out of him. His mouth relaxed in a smile. "Yeah. Let me get Blue's lead."

The puppy sniffed curiously at the leash when Miles attached it to his new harness. He soon forgot about it and dashed out onto the porch to say hello to Pepper.

"Did you have fun with your friends yesterday?" Logan asked as they headed down the steps.

His question made Miles recall exactly what kind of fun he'd had by himself last night and that very morning in the privacy of his bedroom.

"Miles?" Logan said. "You okay?"

Miles flushed at his curious look. "Sorry, my mind was elsewhere. I did, thank you." He paused. "They kept asking me about you after you left."

Logan raised an eyebrow as they started into a low jog. "They did?"

"Yeah." Miles pressed his lips together.

Between Izzy and Hunter's nosiness and Drake and Alex's fatherly attitudes, he'd felt like dinging his friends' ears.

Logan grinned at his expression. "Don't be too hard on them. They're just looking out for you."

His smile made Miles's pulse flutter.

"I know. But I wish they would stop treating me as if I'm going to break." The confession left his mouth before he could stop himself, startling him.

Logan cast a thoughtful look his way as they began pounding the pavement in earnest. "Have you told them that?"

Miles swallowed and shook his head. "It would only hurt their feelings."

Logan was quiet for a while.

"I can see why they're acting the way they are," he said finally. "It must have been hard for them these past twelve years." He glanced at Miles. "They're your best friends, Miles. Not only did they walk out of the accident that put you into a coma, they couldn't help you when you needed them the most. That guilt must have eaten at them every day."

Miles's stomach fell at Logan's words. He looked dazedly at the path.

He'd been so wrapped up in his own thoughts and feelings these past two months, he'd barely tried to see things from the point of view of the people who cherished him.

Have I truly put myself in their shoes since I woke up? Miles clenched his jaw. *And would I have acted any differently if it had been one of them who'd been asleep all this time? If it had been—?* He swallowed convulsively. *If it had been Drake?*

"I'm sorry." Logan slowed and stopped. "I didn't mean to upset you."

Miles halted in his tracks, conscious his emotions had been on full display for Logan to read.

"No." He forced himself to meet Logan's gaze. "You're right. I—" Miles paused and ran a hand through his hair, frustration churning his stomach. "I'm not the greatest when it comes to talking to people. It's probably why my friends always babied me."

"I bet you were a cute baby," Logan said drily.

Miles blinked. Logan's mouth curved in a teasing smile.

Miles's heart lightened. It surprised him how easily Logan could make him forget his worries.

Blue sneezed where he and Pepper were investigating some bushes. Miles guided the curious puppy back onto the curb. He and Logan started running again.

"Tell me more about your friends," Logan said.

To Miles's surprise, he found himself doing just that. Despite what he'd said about not being a great conversationalist, talking with Logan was as easy as breathing.

Logan laughed when Miles described some antics the Terrible Seven had gotten up to when they were kids.

"Carter really ran naked down Main Street when he lost a bet to Hunter?"

"Yup." Miles grinned. "And it was winter to boot. Hunter's dad yelled at us when he came out of his hardware store."

"Carter wasn't there yesterday, right? At your house?"

Miles shook his head. "He's out of town on a shoot right now. God only knows how that player ended up becoming a movie star."

Logan's eyes twinkled. "So, if Carter's the player, what about everyone else?"

Miles counted out on his fingers. "Alex is the sensible one. Hunter's the group's bad boy. Wyatt is the saint. Drake is the wolf. And Tristan's everyone's big brother."

"And Izzy?"

Miles wrinkled his nose. "She's the busybody who wants to see all of us married and pregnant."

Logan chuckled. The sound danced down Miles's spine and made him shiver despite the sun warming his body.

Pain stabbed through his left calf all of a sudden, startling him.

Miles gasped and stumbled to a stop.

Logan sobered and took hold of Miles's shoulder. "What's wrong?" He frowned. "Is it a cramp?"

"Yeah. I get them from time to time." Miles stretched his leg and winced.

Logan looked around.

They were in the park where Miles had found Blue.

"Let's go over there." Logan took Miles's hand and carefully led him to a bench.

Miles's pulse quickened. He glanced nervously at the people walking on the paths and around the lake, and the band playing at the gazebo.

Logan didn't pay them any heed as he sat Miles down. He crouched on the grass in front of the bench and touched Miles's calf.

Miles froze. "What—what are you doing?!"

Logan gave him a puzzled look. "Giving you a massage."

"Oh." Miles bit his lip and did his best to hide his embarrassment.

The way Logan's eyes sparked with amusement told Miles he'd failed miserably. Miles flinched when Logan ran his fingers gently up and down his leg.

"Does that hurt?" Logan asked, his gaze focused on where he was touching Miles.

"A little bit," Miles said in a strangled voice.

Logan's hands stilled. He looked up at Miles. Awareness darkened his eyes to a haunting slate color.

Miles's breath hitched when Logan caressed his sensitive flesh.

"Damn," Logan mumbled.

"What?" Miles breathed, his skin tingling in a way that sent his nerve endings ablaze.

"If you keep looking at me like that, I'm going to do more than massage your leg," Logan said bluntly.

Miles sucked in air, his dick twitching.

Desire brought a flush of color to Logan's cheeks

when he noticed Miles's burgeoning arousal. His gaze burned into Miles's.

"How about we fix this cramp and get you home so we can do something about that?" Logan suggested huskily.

Miles nodded, too dizzy to respond coherently.

The next five minutes were the sweetest torture Miles had ever endured. The feel of Logan's strong fingers expertly kneading his flesh made him want to experience Logan's hands on other parts of his anatomy.

He realized he didn't want Logan to stop touching him.

But he also couldn't wait to find out exactly what Logan intended to do to him once they got home.

Blue and Pepper played close by while Logan gently unknotted the muscles in Miles's leg. Miles dug his nails into his palms and counted the leaves on the grass to curb his erection. From the way Logan clenched his jaw, he was also desperately fighting the attraction heating up the air between them.

"Logan?" Miles mumbled.

"Yeah?"

"I—I think I'm good."

Logan shuddered, his hands stilling on Miles's leg. He rose, took Miles's hand, and led him out of the park, his shoulders stiff and his shuttered expression barely masking his lust.

Miles didn't remember how they got back to the house. All he recalled was the heat of Logan's touch as he clasped Miles's fingers and walked briskly beside him.

Miles's heart thundered in his chest when they finally rounded the bend that led to their homes, the silence between them loaded with so much sexual tension he was finding it hard to breathe.

Logan accelerated his pace.

By the time they made it up the porch of Miles's home, both of them were breathless and flushed.

CHAPTER TEN

Logan waited until Miles closed the door and took Blue's lead off before crowding him against the foyer wall and taking his mouth in a scorching kiss. Blue yipped around their feet before disappearing into the kitchen with Pepper.

Logan parted Miles's lips with a hungry sound and deepened their kiss, his touch urgent where he clasped Miles's face, his expression taut with a passion that made Miles tremble.

Miles closed his eyes and clutched Logan's shoulders as a storm of sensual feelings he'd never experienced flooded his nerve endings. The way Logan's tongue wrapped masterfully around his own was making him lose his grasp on reality. A gasp crowded his throat in the next instant.

Logan had dropped his hands down his back and was clutching his butt. He thrust his hips lightly and ground their groins together.

The feel of Logan's rock-hard erection nudging his own swollen cock had Miles's eyes snapping open.

He shivered when he met Logan's heavy-lidded gaze.

Logan looked like he wanted to eat him alive.

The motion of Logan's tongue slowed as he stared into Miles's dazed eyes, the movements as sinful as the motions of his powerful body where he rocked his hips against Miles's.

The whole thing was so erotic Miles was afraid he would faint.

A protest tumbled from his lips when Logan wrenched their mouths apart.

Logan stared at him hotly. "Where's the closest couch?"

Miles gulped, his breaths coming hard and fast. "There's—there's a den down the hall. It's more private than the living—" The rest of his words were swallowed by Logan's mouth.

Logan ended their kiss, grabbed Miles's hand, and stormed down the hallway. He found the den and tugged Miles's inside. Sunlight streamed through the window looking out over the rear yard and the woods, the golden rays illuminating the cozy room and the faint dust particles in the air.

Logan closed the door, nipped at Miles's lips with his teeth while he backed him to a couch opposite the fireplace, and brought him down on top of him when he sat down. Miles's mouth went dry as he found himself straddling Logan's lap and his raging erection.

"This position will be easier on your leg," Logan said gruffly.

Then his mouth was on Miles's throat and his hands were on Miles's body and the entire world faded away.

Miles could only feel as Logan's lips scorched a hot path down the column of his neck to the frantic pulse beating at the base. A shudder shook him when Logan bit down on his hot flesh. Logan's hands skimmed Miles's chest and back and belly with a featherlight touch that made his flesh twitch and drew a soft moan from his lips.

Miles shivered when Logan's fingers found his nipples. Logan rubbed the hard nubs with the pads of his thumbs. Miles bit his lip.

It felt weird and tingly.

Logan pinched and tugged his nipples.

"Oh!" Miles's eyes rounded at the bolt of sharp pleasure-pain that arrowed through his body all the way to his cock.

Logan looked at him sultrily from under his lashes, a sexy smile playing on his lips. "Do you like that?"

Miles swallowed and nodded shakily. He gasped when Logan kissed his throat and repeated the motion again and again. By the time Logan touched his trembling abs and worked his way to his erection, Miles's nipples were throbbing and he was a hot, quivering mess.

Miles tensed as Logan worked his shorts and boxers down his hips. His face grew hot when his swollen cock sprung free.

Logan cursed at the sight of his engorged flesh and leaking tip. "Shit. Your dick is so pretty."

Air locked in Miles's lungs when Logan skimmed his thumb across the head of his cock and wiped the precum pearling there.

Oh God!

The feel of another man's hand on him felt so exquisite he almost came there and then.

Logan's expression turned feral as he met his dazed gaze. "I can't wait to taste you." He licked his thumb clean.

Miles drew a sharp breath. "That's—that's dirty!" he protested.

Logan grinned wolfishly. "It isn't." He leaned up and kissed Miles.

Heat flooded Miles's face when he tasted his own essence on Logan's tongue. It was so deliciously sinful he wasn't sure where to look.

"None of this is dirty, Miles," Logan murmured against his lips. "And, FYI, I intend to do more debauched things than that to you. But first things first."

Miles barely had time to wonder what Logan meant before Logan reached down and freed his own cock. Miles's eyes widened.

"You're big," he blurted out.

Logan burst out laughing. Miles blushed furiously.

"That's the best compliment I've heard in a long time," Logan chortled. He pressed a torrid kiss to Miles's mouth and ghosted his lips along his cheek to his ear.

Miles shivered and tilted his head to the side when Logan sank his teeth in his lobe.

"Don't worry," Logan whispered hotly. "I'll fit inside you fine. Or—" he teased the shell of Miles's ear with his tongue, "did you want to be inside me?"

Miles squirmed, not knowing if he wanted to run away or grab Logan and never let him go. "Have—have you ever done that?" He moaned when Logan licked and sucked his neck.

"You mean, bottom?" Logan said against his skin.

Miles shivered. "Yeah!"

"No." Logan's tone turned serious as he straightened and met Miles's gaze. "But I wouldn't refuse my partner if that's what they wanted to do."

Miles's belly contracted. Heat flooded his face.

"I—I want you to enter me!"

His breathy confession made Logan curse. Miles choked on his breath when Logan claimed his lips as the same time he took hold of their erections and started stroking.

Miles's fingers sank into Logan's shoulders. He shuddered at the wicked sensations shooting through his flesh. His eyes fluttered closed.

Having someone else do this to him felt a hundred times better than doing it on his own.

His body started moving of its own volition, his hips bucking and shoving his straining erection through Logan's slick grasp.

Logan lifted his mouth off his.

"Look at me," he ordered.

His gravelly tone raised goosebumps on Miles's

skin. Miles blinked his eyes open and met the gaze of the man driving him out of his mind.

Lust stained Logan's cheeks with color. His eyes had turned the shade of a storm-tossed sea, the gray specks within them so bright Miles feared they would scorch him. Delicious tension coiled through Miles's body as Logan stared into his eyes and pleasured him. He panted and gasped and moaned as it built, tightening his back and thighs and knotting his belly.

"You're close." Logan ducked his head and pressed his lips to the column of Miles's throat. "Come for me, Miles."

Blood roared through Miles's skull as the first tendrils of his orgasm stiffened his body. Logan circled his thumb lightly across the sensitive head of his cock. Once. Twice. Three times.

It was all it took to send Miles over the edge.

He cried out as he exploded in Logan's hold, his body jerking and twitching as he convulsed with sweet violence, his cock throbbing and spilling his hot seed inside Logan's hand.

The sounds leaving him were so wanton he could hardly believe he was the one making them.

It was a while before awareness returned.

Miles's head buzzed pleasantly as he blinked. He'd never felt so relaxed and blissfully sated in his entire life. He looked languidly at Logan, only for his breath to catch all over again.

"I was right," Logan said hoarsely. "Your O face is out of this world."

Logan's expression was tight with pleasure as he

stroked himself to his own climax. Miles lowered his gaze. He gulped at the sight of Logan's flushed and straining cock.

Miles reached out and touched Logan.

Logan grunted and jerked.

"I'll come in seconds if you do that," he protested.

Miles shocked himself when he leaned in and nipped at Logan's mouth. "Then, come."

Logan blinked, equally surprised.

Miles stared in Logan's pleasure-glazed eyes and caressed his twitching dick. Logan clenched his jaw. His hands found Miles's thighs, silently granting him the control he longed for.

Miles's heart thundered against his ribs as he took over touching Logan. He explored Logan's throbbing length and the thick veins under his hot skin, his fingers growing more bold. He soon found what Logan liked and began working him steadily.

Logan panted and groaned as Miles stroked him. His neck corded as he neared his climax, his hips rolling and thrusting his cock erratically against Miles's hand. He came on a wild shout, his cum thick and sticky as it anointed Miles's fingers, his hands digging hard into Miles's thighs. He dropped his head on Miles's shoulder and grunted and bucked as he rode the violent waves of his orgasm.

Miles could only watch in wonder, his pulse racing and his chest tight. He didn't think he would ever see anything as beautiful as Logan in the throes of passion.

Logan finally relaxed in his hold, his body shuddering and twitching with aftershocks of pleasure.

Their ragged breathing filled the room as they gazed at one another in the aftermath of their sensual act.

A sultry smile tilted Logan's mouth. "That was incredible."

A wave of shyness danced through Miles and warmed his face. "Really?"

"Yes." Logan chuckled and kissed him. "And I don't think I'll ever tire of that look."

"What look?" Miles mumbled.

Logan grinned and nipped at his throat. "One that says you very much want this big, bad wolf to lick you all over and eat you."

Miles sucked in air, vacillating between mortification and heady anticipation. Mortification won.

"You're—you're terrible!"

Logan laughed at his outraged tone. He leaned back and cocked his head to the side. "So, how was it, Mr. Martinez? Did you enjoy your first non-solo handjob?"

Miles shivered and bit his lip when Logan danced a knuckle down his spent cock. He looked down at the mess they'd made.

"I think the evidence speaks for itself," he said tartly.

Logan stared before snorting. Miles's mouth pressed to a thin line.

"Alright, I'll stop teasing." Logan gave him a kiss that made his entire body tingle. "How about we go clean up and grab breakfast? There's this great little diner I know not far from here."

CHAPTER ELEVEN

Logan came out of his house with Pepper on Friday evening and headed across the road. Lights blazed on the first floor of Miles's home and in a couple of the upstairs windows.

Butterflies swarmed Logan's stomach as he climbed the steps to the porch. He couldn't believe how on edge he was.

Then again, I've never been this serious about a man before.

The way Logan felt toward Miles should have unnerved him. It had been just over two weeks since they'd met. Yet, he couldn't recall being this attracted to another person in his entire life and that included the woman he'd married.

It wasn't just Miles's good looks that had enthralled Logan. He was fascinated by the man himself. Miles had an innocence and a sweetness about him that made Logan want to watch over him. But he also had a strength of will that Logan couldn't help but admire and a sensual side that he loved discovering.

Miles Martinez was an enchanting gift Logan had never expected to find in Twilight Falls and he wanted to unwrap him and get to know him inside and out.

Pepper woofed impatiently as he checked his clothes one last time and pressed the doorbell.

Miles's voice reached him faintly. "Coming!"

Logan's mind was instantly filled with the memory of how Miles had looked when he'd come apart in his arms last Sunday. He cursed under his breath.

Tonight was a first for Miles and he wanted to make sure it was perfect.

His best laid plans flew right out of his head when the door opened.

Logan stared.

Shit. I don't think I'm going to survive the next few hours.

Miles looked like he'd come straight from a catwalk where he stood in his hallway. He was dressed in olive chinos, a light grey dress shirt that brought out the color of his eyes, a navy blazer, and brown leather shoes. A nervous look skittered across his face before he smiled tentatively at Logan, his expensive aftershave tickling Logan's nostrils.

"Hey." Miles's gaze dropped. His eyes widened. "You —you brought flowers?!" he stammered.

Logan shook himself out of the spell he'd fallen under.

"It's your first date." He leaned in, kissed Miles's cheek softly, and handed him the pretty bouquet.

Logan hoped Miles didn't notice the way his hands trembled a little.

Color crept into Miles's cheeks as he accepted the flowers. He buried his face in the blooms to hide his blush. "They're beautiful." He gave Logan a bashful look from under his lashes. "Thank you."

Logan groaned.

Alarm tightened Miles's mouth. "What is it?"

"I'm seriously tempted to skip dinner and feast on you instead," Logan confessed fervently, all notion of staying calm and composed swept away by the adorable storm that was Miles Martinez.

Miles's mouth rounded on a shocked O. "You—you can't! You said you booked an expensive restaurant."

Logan burst out laughing. He pressed a quick peck to Miles's lips. "I don't mind canceling. But I should make good on my promise to you."

Miles chewed his lip, no doubt recalling the conversation they'd had over breakfast on Sunday. "You don't have to do this, you know. It's not like I'm eighteen anymore."

A protective feeling swelled inside Logan at his vulnerable expression.

"I know," he said quietly. "But I want to do this. I want to make all your firsts great, Miles."

Miles's eyes grew misty with emotion.

Logan cursed inwardly. *Yeah, I probably won't make it past dessert.*

"Besides, I went to third base way too fast, so we're going to take it real slow from now on."

Miles's expression fell at Logan's firm tone. "I thought you were joking when you said that."

Logan did his best to keep a straight face at his disappointed mien. "I was dead serious. I'm going to court you properly, Miles Martinez, so no hanky-panky until we have at least two more dates."

Miles looked like a puppy whose favorite toy had just been taken away from him.

"So, does that mean we're really—" He stopped, chewed his lip, and looked around warily before leaning close to Logan, his voice dropping to a whisper despite the fact that there was no one else around, "we're really not going to touch each other's di—!"

Logan pressed a hand to Miles's mouth, not sure whether to laugh or groan.

"You're going to be the death of me," he mumbled. "Come on, let's get out of here before I change my mind and jump you."

Miles's ears went bright red. He went into the kitchen to put the flowers in a vase and returned.

Blue whined when he started closing the door.

Miles stopped, concern clouding his face. "Is he really going to be okay?"

"Yes, he is." Logan leaned down and ruffled the puppy's head. "Pepper's gonna keep you company so be a good boy, Blue," he told the dog firmly.

The puppy wagged his tail slowly. He turned, gave them one last longing look over his shoulder, and padded after Pepper as the hound headed for the kitchen.

Miles locked up and followed Logan to his pickup. "So, where are you taking me?"

Logan smiled and opened the passenger door for Miles. "A place I'm pretty sure you've never been to before."

The way Miles flushed as he climbed inside the vehicle told Logan he appreciated the gentlemanly gesture.

The restaurant Logan drove them to was on the banks of Twilight Falls River, at the end of a secluded driveway a little outside town. From the reviews he'd read online, it served great food and was a favorite among couples.

Miles fingered his blazer when they stepped out of the vehicle.

"Am I dressed alright for this place?"

He stared at the pretty building straddling a verdant rise that rolled gently down to the water.

Logan saw the lines tightening the corners of his eyes and the way his fingers twitched on his clothes. He took Miles's hand and pressed a kiss on the back of his knuckles.

Miles's breath caught, his pupils blowing a little in the dark.

"Yes," Logan assured. "I'm gonna have to beat people off you when we get in there." He skimmed Miles's clothes with a hot gaze. "I forgot to tell you how much I like your outfit. You look amazing, Miles."

Miles flushed at the compliment. "I—Thanks," he mumbled. "My friends went a bit crazy when I came home." He glanced at his clothes. "This is from *Miller,* Theo's store."

"Oh." Logan recalled what Lucy had told him. "He's the one going out with Hunter, right?" He chuckled at Miles's surprised look. "Lucy is the biggest gossip this side of the San Bernardino Mountains."

Miles smiled, his shoulders slowly unknotting. "Yes. Hunter and Theo are engaged."

A maître d'hotel dressed in formal attire greeted them warmly when they entered the foyer. Miles stiffened as they followed him around a partition and entered the main restaurant area. The clink of glasses and cutlery and the sound of muted conversations rose around them as they crossed an elegant dining space with muted lighting.

Logan placed his hand on Miles's lower back and leaned down.

"We're not the only gay couple here, so relax, Miles," he whispered in his ear.

Miles startled before giving him a grateful look.

The maître d'hotel showed them to a reserved table next a window.

Miles gazed at the lights strung across the charming terrace and garden outside as they took their seats. "This place must be beautiful in the summer."

A waiter brought a carafe of water and glasses to their table.

"We should come back next year and see for ourselves," Logan said after the man left.

Miles gave him a blank look.

Logan reached across the table and ran his fingers lightly across the back of Miles's hand.

"I would like to be with you next year too, Miles," he said quietly. "That's if you'll have me."

Logan's heart raced as he met Miles's dazed stare. He'd thought he hadn't been ready for a serious relationship. Yet here he was, trying to convince a man he met less than a month ago that he wanted them to do just that.

It was shocking and unexpected. But, more than anything, it felt…right. Like it was meant to be.

Logan knew he wanted this more than he'd ever wanted anything in his entire adult life.

Miles swallowed at what he saw on Logan's face. "I'd—I'd like that very much." He pulled his hand away, opened the à la carte menu, and hid behind it, his ears bright red and his eyes sparkling with happiness.

Logan stifled a groan.

I'm seriously going to break that promise I made about not touching him if he gets any cuter than this.

"Miles?" someone said in a startled voice.

CHAPTER TWELVE

Miles froze. His pulse quickened as he lowered the menu and stared at the couple who'd stopped by their table.

It was Wyatt and Nathan.

What are they doing here?!

"Hi, Wyatt," Logan said calmly.

"Logan," Wyatt greeted distractedly. He couldn't fully mask his surprise as his gaze returned to Miles. "I wasn't sure if it was you at first."

"Hey, Wyatt," Miles said awkwardly. "Hi, Nathan."

"Miles." Nathan's eyes twinkled as he studied Miles and Logan. "Are you going to introduce me to your…?"

"Date," Logan stated steadily. He took Miles's hand.

Wyatt's eyes widened.

Miles's stomach clenched. He met Logan's encouraging gaze and set his jaw in a determined line.

"Nathan, this is Logan Prescott, my date. Logan, this is Nathan Hardy, Wyatt's fiancé."

Nathan smiled at Logan. "Wyatt told me about you."

Logan's expression grew amused.

Wyatt looked like he was contemplating crawling under a table.

"Do you guys usually dine here?" Logan said curiously.

"This is where Wyatt brought me on our first date." Nathan's smile widened. "We're celebrating our six-month anniversary." A mischievous light dawned on his face. He leaned down, his voice dropping to a loud whisper. "We're also celebrating the first time he made me come with his—"

Wyatt groaned, clamped a hand over Nathan's mouth, and dragged him away. "Enjoy your date," he called out over his shoulder.

Miles could tell from his expression that he truly meant that. He'd just started to unwind when Nathan returned to their table.

"We're going for drinks at *The Watering Hole* later. Care to join us?"

Logan looked at Miles and arched an eyebrow. "I don't mind."

Miles chewed his lip. He'd been to the bar a few times with the Terrible Seven. Though he liked the place and the atmosphere, he sometimes felt like all eyes were on him when he went there.

He chided himself. Tonight wasn't just about him.

Miles met Logan's gaze steadily. "Okay."

The waiter returned with a basket of fresh bread and took their order. "Would you like some wine with your dinner?"

"I'm driving, so I'll just have water. But he can drink." Logan indicated Miles.

Miles hesitated before taking the wine list the waiter handed him. He stared at the names on the menu. Bar the rosé his mom used to give him at Christmas, he knew next to nothing about wines.

"The Cabernet Sauvignon will go well with your meal," Logan suggested.

Miles could tell from his contrite look that he'd realized his faux pas. He flashed a grateful half-smile his way. "Thanks." He handed the list to the waiter. "I'll have a small glass of that please."

Logan waited until the waiter left before reaching over and linking his fingers with Miles. "I'm sorry. That was ignorant of me."

"It's okay." Miles found himself liking the casual way Logan touched him. "Besides, I suspect if we'd done this a decade ago, neither of us would have known what anything on that list was."

Logan smiled. "And we would have bluffed our way through it somehow and gotten stone drunk in the process."

Miles chuckled, the knots in his shoulders finally loosening.

Logan's expression softened. "Feeling better?"

"Yeah." Miles hesitated. "Thank you for doing this. I know I said I didn't need any of it, but—" he looked around the restaurant, butterflies swarming his belly for the first time that evening, "it's only now sinking in that I'm doing something really special tonight. And I'm glad it's with you."

Logan's hand twitched around Miles's fingers. His eyes darkened.

"I want to kiss you so bad right now," he confessed, not bothering to hide his desire.

Miles laughed. Logan's expression turned predatory.

Miles's heartbeat picked up as sexual tension oozed between them. He shivered when Logan rubbed the pad of his thumb over the pulse racing at his wrist.

"Your skin's getting hot," Logan said huskily.

Miles's cock stirred at his burning gaze. "And whose fault is that?"

Logan pursed his lips and sighed. "It's mine." He reluctantly released Miles's hand. "Sticking to that three-date rule is gonna hurt." He looked down. "Little Logan was really rearing to go there."

Miles blushed. "I can't believe you gave it a name. And there's nothing little about it."

Logan chuckled. "You mean, you haven't given yours a name?" His tone was one hundred percent tease. "Miles Junior sounds pretty—"

Luckily, the waiter returned with Miles's wine and their starters before Miles could figure out a way to make Logan shut up.

Dinner was surprisingly fun and not just because of the food. Miles found himself chatting with Logan like they'd known each all their lives. Logan told him about growing up in Sacramento, his family and his whirlwind marriage, and how he'd realized he was into guys.

Surprise jolted Miles when Logan told him about

his first sexual encounter with a man. "It was a one-night stand?"

Logan shrugged. "I wanted to know if I could get hard with a guy. We were pretty open with each other before we went to the hotel. I told him I had never had sex with a man. He didn't mind."

Finding out Logan had opted to have a one-night stand for his first experience with a man made Miles feel strange. He wasn't completely certain what name to give to the hot sensation tightening his stomach.

Was he judging Logan for having sex with someone he hadn't cared for? Or was he annoyed Logan's first time had been with a stranger and not—

—*me*. Miles froze, startled. *Wait. Am I—am I jealous?!*

"You have a really weird look on your face right now," Logan said.

"Sorry." Miles bit his lip.

"I'll be honest with you, it wasn't the only one-night stand I had," Logan said quietly. "I dated a few guys before I left Sacramento, but they were sex friends more than partners." He paused. "I'm not ashamed of that. It made me realize I had a pretty healthy sex drive."

Unease coiled through Miles.

"So, you've done this before?" He indicated the restaurant.

Logan raised an eyebrow. "You mean, give flowers to a guy and wine and dine him?" The smile that stretched his mouth raised goosebumps on Miles's skin. "No, Miles. I don't do this kind of thing with sex friends." He propped his elbows on the table and leaned in close. "I've never done any of this with another man."

Miles's heart tingled at his heated gaze. "Oh."

He did his best to stifle a goofy smile.

Logan's eyes darkened with emotion. He took Miles's hand and kissed the back of his knuckles.

"I would only ever do this with someone I'm serious about." Logan turned Miles's wrist over and pressed his lips to his racing pulse. "I meant it when I said I fully intend to court you, Miles."

Miles nearly melted in a puddle of goo at his words.

From the misty glances they earned from a few of the tables around them, the other diners had overheard their conversation. A choked off wolf-whistle came from the opposite side of the restaurant.

Logan looked around and snorted. Miles sighed.

Wyatt was doing his best to drag Nathan back into his chair.

"I can't believe those guys are my friends," Miles muttered.

"Admit it," Logan said with a grin. "You wouldn't have them any other way."

Miles's chest tightened. "You're right. I wouldn't."

Logan squeezed his fingers at the way his voice trembled a little.

CHAPTER THIRTEEN

LOGAN PARKED NEXT TO WYATT'S SUV. HE TURNED THE engine off and climbed out of the pickup with Miles. They joined Wyatt and Nathan and headed for the charming gray and white clapboard building on the other side of the parking lot.

A pink neon sign above the front door proclaimed the name of the bar.

Logan observed the crowded parking bays. "I didn't expect it to be this full even on a Friday night."

"It's popular with regular folks too," Nathan explained. He glanced at his fiancé. "I have some pretty fun memories of this place when Wyatt and I started going out."

Wyatt sighed at Nathan's wicked little smile.

Logan had been surprised when Miles had related how Wyatt and Nathan had gotten together on the drive back into town. Nathan had been straight and had even been engaged to be married before he got into a road traffic accident that almost crippled him.

The incident had changed Nathan's outlook on almost everything in his life. He'd broken off his engagement to the woman he'd thought he'd loved and abandoned the dazzling career he'd spent years building.

After drifting around for a while doing contract jobs, Nathan had come to Twilight Falls to work for Wyatt's web and graphic design company. According to Izzy, Wyatt had a crush on Nathan for the longest time before they finally became a couple. And it was Nathan who'd made the first move.

Miles's friends really are incredible.

Heat and the noise of a lively crowd washed over Logan when he entered the bar with the three men. He could immediately tell why *The Watering Hole* was so popular.

The soft lighting and dark wood furniture lent an air of sophistication to the bar that wouldn't have looked out of place in a big city. Yet it managed to be warm and welcoming at the same time.

Logan could tell a lot of money had been spent on the decor and the furnishings. He caught a glimpse of a back room with a glittering disco ball over the heads of the men and women filling the main area.

"This place has a dance floor?"

"Yup," Nathan drawled. "Don't let Hunter drag you on there. You'll never escape."

"Don't," Miles groaned. "I'm getting flashbacks to when he forced me to dance with him a month ago."

Logan smiled. "You got moves I need to see, Mr. Martinez?"

"I have moves," Miles muttered. "I'm not sure you really want to see them."

"He has two left feet," Nathan said teasingly.

"*I* have two left feet," Wyatt grunted. "Compared to me, Miles is practically a swan."

Logan chuckled. He caught a few curious glances aimed their way as they made their way through the throng of people. Miles tensed a little beside him.

"Are you okay?" Logan said, puzzled.

"Yeah." Miles made a face. "I'm…not really good with crowds." His shoulder brushed Logan's arm as he drew closer to him.

Logan's heart swelled. He placed a firm hand on Miles's lower back.

Miles startled. He flushed at the look Logan gave him.

"Why don't we find somewhere quiet after we get out drinks?" Logan suggested.

Miles nodded and swallowed.

Wyatt's expression turned complicated when he saw the proprietary way Logan was touching Miles. "Yeah, I think you can forget that idea." He indicated something on the other side of the bar.

"Yoohoo!" a man shouted jovially from across the room.

Logan stared. It was Hunter. He wasn't alone.

Miles's face fell at the sight of the men seated around three tables that had been pushed together.

"Did you know they'd be here?" he asked Nathan accusingly.

"Nope."

They got their drinks and made their way over. Hunter had already magicked extra chairs from somewhere. Logan registered several new faces as he approached, including a couple he'd only ever seen on TV.

Carter Wilson observed Logan curiously when Miles took the seat next to the handsome man with chocolate brown eyes and honey-colored skin beside him. Miles started making introductions.

Elijah Davis-Wilson addressed Logan warmly. "It's nice to meet you. Miles told me you were a great help to him. I'm glad you're his new neighbor."

Logan shook the pastry chef's hand and sat beside Miles. "It's nice to meet you too."

He could guess why Miles and Elijah had hit it off and become good friends. The chef had a soothing presence.

"You're back from your shoot," Miles told Carter.

Carter grimaced. "It's only a short break. I'm leaving town again next week."

Lines wrinkled Miles's brow. "Will you be here for Christmas?"

"Yes." Carter's expression softened as he gazed at Elijah. "I wouldn't miss Christmas with my husband and my daughter for the whole world." He smiled at Miles. "And you. This Christmas is going to be extra special."

Elijah clasped his husband's hand.

Emotion darkened Miles's eyes.

Logan knew being with his friends for the

festivities for the first time in over a decade would mean the world to him too.

Miles introduced the rest of the men.

Logan nodded to James Lang and Finn West. "Hi."

Finn nodded back. "Hi." He indicated the sappy-faced Carter and Elijah with his beer bottle. "Sorry about the PDA. You'll get used to it."

"Hey," James greeted a little guardedly.

Tristan dipped his chin at Logan. The mechanic looked more at ease than the last time they'd met.

Roman Campbell welcomed Logan with a friendly smile.

The man beside the rockstar studied Logan warily.

"Drake," Logan said lightly.

"Logan," Drake muttered.

Alex rolled his eyes. "How about you put your caveman attitude away?"

Logan did his best to keep a straight face as Drake's expression soured. Roman glanced quizzically at his fiancé.

"What's the matter with him?" Finn asked Alex.

"Papa Bear doesn't like the fact that Baby Bear found a new playmate," the lawyer said acerbically.

This statement earned Logan and Miles a battery of stares. Miles flushed. Drake frowned.

"It's best to ignore them when they get like this," Theo Miller drawled. He shook Logan's hand. "I hope Hunter didn't say anything too horrific the other day."

Hunter sucked in air and pressed a hand to his chest. "How could you say that about your beloved husband-to-be?"

Theo kissed his cheek. "That's because I know you." His eyes twinkled. "It's a good thing I love you. Anyone else would have muzzled you by now."

Hunter straightened in his seat, interest brightening his gaze.

Theo narrowed his eyes at his fiancé. "I'm not buying you a muzzle for sex play."

"Jesus," Wyatt mumbled.

Nathan chortled. Logan grinned.

"You could always get him a ball and gag," Roman suggested with a straight face.

Drake almost dropped his drink.

James lowered his brows at Roman. "How about you not reveal the details of your private life to everyone? I get that you and Yogi Bear over there can barely get out of the bedroom most days, but we're in a public place, so behave."

"Yogi—Yogi Bear!" Hunter snorted while Drake's frown turned positively murderous.

Roman stuck his tongue out at James.

"Seriously, it's like being with a bunch of five-year olds," Alex muttered.

Finn chuckled.

"What are you guys talking about?" someone said behind Logan.

Logan turned.

Izzy was taking her scarf and coat off. She dropped them on the back of her brother's chair and grabbed a vacant stool from another table.

"I thought you were out with Sam and Imogen," Wyatt said.

"I was. They called it a night. I thought at least one of you would be at your favorite hunting ground." She gave Logan a curious half-smile. "Hey. I wasn't expecting to see you here."

"Logan and Miles are on a date," Nathan said before Logan could reply.

Miles stiffened. Hunter gaped.

A shocked silence descended around the table.

Wyatt pinched the bridge of his nose. "Time and place, Nathan."

"What?" Nathan shrugged. "They were going to find out anyway." He arched an eyebrow at Logan, his expression teasing. "Besides, better to face the music now than get stabbed in the back later."

Miles bristled at his words.

"He's joking," Elijah reassured.

Logan could tell from a few faces around the table that not everyone was thrilled at this news. Some of the color had drained from Izzy's face. She was staring at him and Miles with the strangest expression.

Logan steeled himself. Having to deal with the Terrible Seven would put the fear of God into almost anyone. Another man might have turned tail and ran out of the bar.

But Logan wasn't just another man. He took hold of Miles's hand.

Time to make some things clear.

"Like Nathan said, Miles and I have decided to date," he told the men and woman watching him calmly. "I hope you'll come to accept me in your circle."

Miles shot a grateful look at Logan. He squared his

shoulders and met his friends' stunned stares. "Logan is right. We're dating."

"Isn't it a bit too soon for you to be going out with someone?" Drake said stiffly in the fraught hush. "You've only just come out of your—"

"It isn't." Miles's voice turned brittle. "My life has been on hold for twelve whole years, Drake. I can't stay frozen in the past forever." His fingers trembled a little in Logan's hand. "I like Logan." He gazed at Logan. "He…makes me feel alive in a way I haven't felt in a really long time."

CHAPTER FOURTEEN

Logan's chest tightened at Miles's confession and
the wealth of emotions glittering in his beautiful eyes.
He could tell the words Miles had just spoken shocked
Izzy and the Terrible Seven.

"Then, I'm happy for you," Alex said quietly.

A soft smile stretched Wyatt's mouth. "Yeah."

Tristan's gaze swung from Logan to Miles. "You
guys look good together," he grunted.

"More to the point, those clothes really suit you,"
Theo told Miles with a warm smile. "I'm glad you
picked them for your date."

"Thanks." Miles's ears reddened a little.

Logan turned to Theo, his expression deadpan.

"Thank *you*. I'm really looking forward to taking
them off him later."

Theo blinked. Miles sucked in air. Hunter almost
fell out of his chair. James's eyes rounded a little behind
his glasses. Carter's jaw dropped open.

"I like this guy!" Roman chortled.

Finn and Nathan's shoulders trembled at Drake's outraged expression. Wyatt and Elijah smiled into their drinks. Tristan and Alex studied Logan with newfound respect.

"I was kidding," Logan told a red-faced Miles before he could melt into an embarrassed puddle. "We're sticking to the three-date rule."

"Yeah, good luck with that," Roman snorted.

"You're terrible," Miles grumbled at Logan.

Logan grinned and pressed a soft kiss his temple. "I'm looking forward to making you blush even harder than you are right now, Mr. Martinez," he whispered in his ear.

Miles groaned into his drink.

Logan excused himself to go to the rest room a while later.

Drake was waiting for him when he came out.

"Can we talk?" Drake said gruffly.

Logan raised an eyebrow. "Is this an ambush?" He looked up and down the passage. "Are the rest of the guys about to spring out and rough me up?"

Drake made an exasperated sound. "You know, that smart mouth is part of the reason I don't like you."

"So, what do you want to talk about?" Logan said mildly.

He could tell his tone ticked Drake off even more.

"Not here." Drake turned and headed for a back door. "Follow me."

Logan glanced toward the main bar before reluctantly falling in his footsteps.

They came out on a terrace that overlooked a

seating area and a garden. Drake walked over to the porch railing and braced his hands on the banister.

Logan saw a muscle work in his cheek as he gazed at the dark mountains rising in the distance.

"What do you want to tell me, Drake?"

Drake took a deep breath and turned to meet Logan's gaze.

"You need to stop hanging out with Miles."

Irritation tightened Logan's jaw. He forced himself to relax.

"And why is that?"

"Because he's too vulnerable right now." Drake lowered his brows. "Did he tell you about the accident?"

"He did," Logan said calmly. He crossed the porch and rested a shoulder against the post beside Drake. "I know he was in a coma and only woke up two months ago."

Drake's expression hardened. "Then you must know Miles isn't in his right mind. He's still..." He straightened and ran a hand through his hair, frustration etched in the lines of his face. "He's still confused, okay? So you should back off and leave him—"

"No."

Drake flinched. "What?"

Logan sighed. "You guys are behaving like idiots. Then again, I can't entirely blame you."

Drake turned to glare at him, his hands fisting at his sides.

"What the hell do you mean by that?!" he snapped.

"All of you are in so deep you can barely see the woods for the trees," Logan replied steadily. "You're treating Miles with kids gloves. Like he's something precious that you have to protect at all costs. You'll lose him if you keep acting like he's gonna break the minute you say or do the wrong thing."

Drake recoiled.

Remorse churned Logan's insides at his haunted look. He grimaced and rubbed the back of his neck.

"Look, I know where you're coming from. I really do. You and your friends only want the best for Miles. You want him to be happy. And he will be. But you need to give him space to breathe. You need to let him fall and pick himself back up again. Miles *is* lost right now. But that doesn't mean he doesn't know what he wants."

"And he wants you?" Drake said harshly. "Is that what you're saying?"

"Yes." Though Logan knew his words sounded harsh, he was conscious Drake needed to hear them. "Right now, Miles needs someone who isn't mired in the past. He's trying to find a way to live again. Even though you want nothing more than to help him, your history together means you're holding him back." He hesitated. "Whether you like it or not Drake, you and your friends are smothering him with your emotions. And he's drowning because he wants to meet your expectations and make you happy, but he's losing sight of who he really is in the process."

Drake swallowed and closed his eyes briefly, his

expression pained. "Did he say that to you?" he said after a short silence.

"He didn't. But I'm beginning to know Miles enough to guess what he's thinking." Logan met Drake's accusing gaze unflinchingly. "I can't even begin to imagine what it must have been like for the rest of you all these years," he said quietly. "How you must have grieved every time you went to see him. How…guilty you must have felt that you walked out of that accident and he didn't."

Drake shuddered and dropped his gaze to the ground. "I—shit!" He pressed his knuckles to his eyes. "You really know how to kick a guy when he's already down, don't you?"

Logan shrugged. "Yeah, my ex-wife used to tell me that."

Drake froze. "Wait. You were *married*?!" he asked, aghast.

"For a good few years. I got divorced when I realized I was gay."

Drake narrowed his eyes. "Miles isn't some kind of project for you, is he? You're not fooling around with him just so you can satisfy your curiosity?"

This time, Logan did nothing to mask his annoyance. "It's a good thing you're Miles's friend or I would have punched you for that stupid question," he said in a hard voice. "I like Miles, Drake. A lot more than I ever thought I would like another person, man or woman."

Drake stared, surprise widening his eyes a little. "Are you saying you're falling in love with him?"

Logan stilled. His pulse quickened.

Am I falling in love with Miles?!

Whatever Drake saw on Logan's face made his expression ease. "You don't have to answer that," he said gruffly. He looked out over the mountains and sighed. "And thank you. For being there for him." He flashed a warning glance at Logan. "You better make him happy."

"I will." Logan propped his elbows on the railing. "I promise."

Drake hunched down beside him. "And you better, you know, not hurt him," he muttered.

Logan gave him a quizzical look.

Drake made a face. "I mean, during sex. Miles is a virgin, isn't he?"

Logan bit his lip hard at Drake's conflicted expression. "He is," he finally managed without laughing. "Although the guy's doing his damndest to lose that particular tag."

Drake drew a sharp breath.

Logan grinned at his incensed look. "If Miles had his own way, I would have popped his cherry by now. I'm the one who insisted we take things slow. I want to make sure his first time is unforgettable for all the right reasons."

Drake glowered at him for a moment before dropping his head in his hands. His shoulders sagged.

"Is it alright if I still think you're a giant asshole despite what you just said?" he groaned.

Logan chuckled and patted him on the shoulder.

"Don't worry. I'm sure you'll be adding the word lovable to that sentence soon."

"I don't know about that," Drake grunted. "We should head back. Miles will be wondering where you are."

They returned to the bar.

"I'm gonna get another round of drinks," Drake said. "You want anything?"

"I'm good, thanks."

Drake headed over to the counter while Logan made his way through the crowd to their table. Miles brightened when he spotted him.

Logan's steps slowed.

Though she'd done her best to appear composed so far, Izzy wasn't able to completely conceal her emotions as she stole a glance at Miles from under her lashes.

Logan's heart sank. He finally understood what he'd read on her face when Nathan had told everyone Miles and him were dating.

Izzy liked Miles.

And it seemed Miles was completely unaware of this fact.

CHAPTER FIFTEEN

Izzy was still on Logan's mind when Miles pulled up outside the Batistas' home the following Wednesday. He hadn't told Miles about his suspicions when he'd taken him home last Friday.

Izzy had evidently decided to keep her feelings a secret for a reason.

Is it because she realized Miles was gay? Or did she not want to jeopardize their friendship?

Since worrying about the issue wasn't going to achieve anything, Logan decided to enjoy his evening. He studied the gaily decorated house as Miles switched the engine off.

"This is nice."

There were several cars and pickups parked on the driveway, along with a black Harley.

"Drake is here," Miles muttered.

Logan looked around at his uneasy tone.

Miles was chewing his lip as he stared at the motorbike.

"What's wrong?" Logan asked.

Miles hesitated before meeting his gaze. "Are you sure you're okay being here? My friends were rude to you the other day, especially Drake." His fingers flexed on the steering wheel. "I know Wyatt invited you to poker night, but we don't have to go in if you don't want to."

Logan's lips stretched in a soft smile at his troubled expression. "I have pretty thick skin, Miles. And your friends don't scare me. They're all bark and zero bite." He leaned over and kissed the tip of Miles's nose. "Besides, Drake and I had a talk last week."

"You did?" Miles's eyes rounded. "When?!"

"He was waiting for me outside the rest room at *The Watering Hole*."

Miles furrowed his brow. "He didn't threaten you, did he?"

"We talked." Logan squeezed his hand. "He cares about you, Miles, so go easy on him."

Miles swallowed, his expression still dark.

Logan decided kissing him would make a good distraction. Miles stiffened as he swooped in and claimed his mouth.

The way he closed his eyes and melted into Logan with his next breath made Logan want to get behind the wheel, drive them home, and take Miles upstairs to his bedroom.

Logan shuddered and ended the kiss, only to curse when he saw Miles's face.

"Don't look at me like that."

Miles touched his lips with trembling fingers.

"Don't look at you like what?" he mumbled dazedly.

Logan kept his hands to himself by a sheer act of will. "Like you want me to strip you naked and take you, right here, right now."

Miles went beetroot red at his husky words.

Logan sighed, crossed his forearms on the dashboard, and dropped his forehead atop them. "You're gonna be the death of me, Miles Martinez," he groaned. "I can feel it in my bones."

"You're the one who insisted on the three-date rule," Miles protested.

A sharp knock came at Miles's window, startling them both.

It was Tristan.

James had climbed off the powerful black and silver Harley parked in front of them and was taking his helmet off.

Logan swallowed a sigh.

Christ, I can't believe we didn't even hear their motorbike.

"Are you guys coming in?" Tristan said through the glass, his face puzzled.

"We—we are," Miles replied, flustered.

"We will as soon as I get on top of this erection," Logan muttered under his breath.

Miles hushed him.

"Why don't you go on ahead?" he told Tristan. "We'll be there in a second."

Tristan nodded and disappeared.

Logan exited the vehicle with Miles a short while later, his groin less tight in the confines of his jeans.

Pepper and Blue jumped out of the back seat when Miles opened the rear door and started sniffing around Wyatt and Izzy's front yard.

Wyatt appeared in the entrance when they reached the porch. "You made it." He smiled when Blue and Pepper came over to greet him and bent down to ruffle their heads. "Thanks for bringing the dogs. Maisie's gonna go bananas when she sees them." He straightened and stood aside. "Come on in."

The sweet smell of sugar and spice teased Logan's nose when he entered the house with Miles and the dogs. He looked around curiously as Wyatt took their coats and put them in a closet.

A giant Christmas tree decked with lights and baubles dominated a pretty living room visible through an arched doorway on the right. The wall on the left of the hall was covered in picture frames.

Logan wandered over to take a closer look.

The Terrible Seven featured in several of the photographs, their faces bright as they beamed at the camera. The pictures showed them from when they were toothy little troublemakers with scuffed knees all the way to when they became gangly teenagers.

Logan's chest tightened a little.

Miles had barely changed. He wore a quiet, shy smile in most of the pictures despite the fact that he was surrounded by his friends.

I wonder if he realizes they were looking out for him, even then?

Logan reluctantly dragged his gaze from the photographs. "You and Izzy live here?"

"Yeah." Wyatt guided them down the passage toward the source of the lively voices filling the house. "We split the upstairs into two wings after our parents left."

They entered a large kitchen that looked out over a backyard festooned with Christmas lights. Most of the Terrible Seven and their significant other were crowded around the table in the middle of the room.

Alex cooked chicken nuggets and fries at the range while Finn made a salad.

Elijah was putting the finishing touches to an apple pie.

The pastry chef smiled warmly when he saw them. He wiped his hands on a kitchen towel and came over to hug Miles.

"Hey."

"Hi, Elijah." Miles sobered at the sight of Drake.

"Miles," Drake said quietly. He bobbed his head graciously at Logan. "It's good to see you, Logan."

Everyone stared. Even Roman gave his fiancé a blank look.

"Who are you and what did you do with the real Drake?" Hunter said suspiciously.

"Ha-ha," Drake grumbled.

Logan caught the surprised glance Miles aimed his way. He leaned over.

"See? I told you I tamed Yogi Bear," Logan whispered in Miles's ear.

Miles swallowed a laugh.

Logan found himself the focus of a pair of bright blue eyes. A little girl with blonde hair stared at him inquisitively from Carter's lap. Her eyes rounded when Blue and Pepper entered the kitchen.

"Doggies!" she squealed.

Carter held on to her as she made to bolt from his knee. "Remember what we said, Maisie. You need to be gentle so you don't scare them."

Maisie bit her lip and nodded. Carter carefully put her on the floor.

Logan squatted between the dogs and placed his hands on their necks to keep them still.

"Come say hello to Blue and Pepper, Maisie," he said with a smile.

Maisie headed over, her eyes sparkling. Pepper wagged her tail as the little girl softly stroked her head and back. Blue sniffed Maisie's hand hesitantly. He started licking her fingers with slobbery enthusiasm, his tail beating so fast it blurred.

Maisie giggled and squirmed. "That tickles!"

"Who wants to tell her Blue is probably after the hot dog he can taste on her fingers," Hunter whispered.

Theo hushed him.

Maisie looked at Logan. "Are you Uncle Miles's friend?" she asked with the innocent curiosity of a four-year old.

"I am," Logan replied lightly.

Hunter smirked. "He's his *special—Ouch!*"

Nathan had jabbed an elbow in his ribs.

Miles narrowed his eyes at Hunter.

"You should buy that muzzle," James told Theo.

Maisie's gaze swung to Miles and back. "I'm gonna marry Uncle Miles when I'm all grown up."

Logan tried hard not to laugh at Miles's mortified face. He arched an eyebrow at the little girl. "You are?"

Maisie bobbed her head. "Ah-huh."

Roman grinned and tipped his beer bottle at Logan. "Looks like you have competition."

Izzy came into the kitchen just as Wyatt took home-made pizzas out of the oven. Her shoulders tightened a little when she saw Miles and Logan seated at the table.

"Hey," she murmured, pasting a smile across her face.

Logan noted the way she carefully avoided his gaze.

Maisie sneaked food to the two dogs under the table throughout dinner and giggled every time they licked her fingers. Though the conversation flowed easily, Logan was conscious Izzy avoided talking to him directly.

Miles and the others didn't seem to notice.

Elijah bowed out of playing poker and headed into the den with Maisie and the dogs. Miles and Izzy joined them a short while later.

Logan ended up winning the game.

It took him a moment to realize the other men were staring at him with bemused expressions as he gathered his cards. "What?"

"James normally beats us at poker," Drake said.

"Although it's often a close call between him and Tristan," Alex remarked.

"Tristan used to win before James came into the picture," Hunter explained with a smirk.

"Ah." Logan made a face at James and Tristan. "Sorry."

"It's alright," James grunted. "I'll beat your ass next week."

"Babe," Tristan muttered with a chagrined look while chuckles broke out around the table.

Logan grinned. "Challenge accepted." He offered James his hand.

James grumbled and shook it.

Nathan stood up. "Better make coffee to go with that pie."

Wyatt accompanied him and uncovered the pie on the cooling rack on the counter.

Hunter sniffed the air appreciatively as the heady smell of baked apples and cinnamon filled the room. "I swear, eating Elijah's food is as close as I can get to an orgasm outside the bedroom."

This elicited groans from everyone. Theo sighed.

"I'll buy you the damn muzzle for Christmas," James told Hunter's fiancé with a scowl.

Logan chuckled and rose to go check up on Miles and the dogs. He froze when he stepped inside the hall.

Izzy was slipping out the front door.

Logan's mood sobered. He'd briefly forgotten about the whole Izzy conundrum. He hesitated before heading for the door.

Logan wasn't sure why he was going after Izzy. He just knew he couldn't leave things as they were between them. Not when he intended to be a big part of Miles's life.

Logan slowed when he passed the den. His chest lightened.

Elijah had changed Maisie into pajamas and was cradling her in his lap on the floor, in front of a roaring fire. Miles sat in front of them and read the sleepy little girl a story, the dogs lying quietly next to him.

Logan smiled and strolled into the foyer. He spotted the blankets sitting on the lower shelf of a console table and grabbed a pair before he went outside.

CHAPTER SIXTEEN

ELIJAH'S VOICE FADED BEHIND MILES AS HE STEPPED OUT into the hallway. He'd taken over telling Maisie a bedtime story so Miles could go to the rest room.

Miles swallowed a sigh.

He still wasn't sure how he felt about Logan coming over for poker night.

It was only after Logan had dropped him home at the end of their date last Friday and pressed a chaste kiss to his cheek before bidding him goodnight, that Miles had realized a startling truth.

He wasn't ready to share Logan with his friends yet.

Guilt tightened his belly at that thought.

Jeez, who knew I could be so selfish.

A cold draft raised goosebumps on his neck. He turned in time to see Logan disappear out the front door with a pair of blankets.

Miles frowned. He faltered before retracing his steps, curious as to what Logan was up to.

The door was slightly ajar when he entered the

foyer. He was about to pull it open when he heard Izzy's voice.

❧

Izzy startled when Logan appeared on the porch. "Oh."

"Hey." Logan walked over and handed her a blanket.

Izzy hesitated before accepting it. "Thanks." She wrapped it around her shoulders where she stood at the railing.

Logan did the same and followed her gaze to the soft lights in the distance.

"I'm sorry," Izzy said after a short silence.

"For what?"

Izzy sighed and hung her head. She turned and leaned her back against the banister. "I'm aware I've been acting like a bitch." She wrinkled her nose at him. "Just so you know, it isn't personal. I'll be back to my normal, cheery self soon."

"I'm glad to hear that," Logan said quietly.

He hesitated. *Might as well go for broke.*

"Why did you never tell him that you liked him?"

Izzy's eyes flared at his question. She bit her lip. "Was it that obvious?" she mumbled.

"Not really." Logan shrugged. "I'm just good at reading people."

Izzy took a shallow breath and closed her eyes briefly. "I've liked Miles since I was in high school." She twisted around and stared blindly at the distant town lights. "He came out of the closet the same year I realized I had the biggest crush on him. There wasn't much point saying anything after that."

"You still like him," Logan stated, matter-of-fact.

Izzy grimaced. "To be honest, I'm pretty sure I'm just crushing hard." Her expression turned haunted. "I held on to a stupid dream after the accident." Her voice trembled slightly. "For some reason, I thought he'd wake up one day and, well…see me. Not Izzy, the little girl who followed him around when she was a kid, but Izzy, the grown woman who desired him." Her eyes glittered as she glanced at Logan. "Isn't that utterly foolish?"

Logan faltered before patting her back softly. "To be honest, it's not the dumbest thing I've heard lately."

"Thanks, I think." Izzy sniffed and leaned her head on his shoulder. "So, have you guys had sex yet?"

Logan choked on a snort. "Umm, no."

"Why not?" She squinted at him. "Do you have a performance issue?"

Logan chuckled. "I'm not impotent if that's what you're worried about." He gazed out into the night and smiled wistfully before meeting her curious stare. "It's because I want to make all of Miles's firsts perfect."

Izzy stared at him like he'd grown another head. "Dammit," she said, annoyed. "You make it really hard to hate you, Logan Prescott, you know that?"

Logan grinned. "I'm sorry to disappoint."

IZZY ROLLED HER EYES. "JUST MAKE SURE YOU PREP Miles well before you stick your loaded gun in him. I'd hate to see him all hunched up and shuffling like an old man after you do the dirty deed."

Logan burst out laughing. Izzy smiled.

MILES'S HEART THUMPED VIOLENTLY AGAINST HIS CHEST. He stepped silently away from the door.

Izzy—Izzy likes me?!

He headed into the rest room in a daze, only to flinch when he saw himself in the mirror above the sink.

He looked flushed, like he had a fever.

Miles opened the faucet and splashed cold water on his face, his mind spinning from what he'd just heard. One thing kept resonating through his mind.

Logan had somehow guessed that Izzy liked him. Yet he himself had failed to see it, even though he'd known her practically his whole life.

Miles clenched his jaw and bunched his fists on the edge of the basin, regret a heavy weight in the pit of his stomach.

Does anyone else know? Does—does Wyatt?!

Miles squeezed his eyes shut.

Just like Logan, he doubted Wyatt would have said anything even if he knew. Izzy's secret was hers to keep. And, judging from what Miles had accidentally overheard, she never intended to reveal it.

Miles wasn't sure how he made it through the rest

of that evening. He was conscious Logan had picked up on his mood and kept casting worried glances his way when no one else was looking. Relief almost made him giddy when they left Wyatt and Izzy's house just after ten.

"Logan?" he mumbled as they walked down the driveway.

"Yeah?"

"Do you mind driving?"

Logan frowned slightly. "Of course not."

He took the car keys off Miles and got behind the steering wheel.

They rode back in silence, Miles gazing blindly out of the window most of the way. It took a moment for him to register that they'd reached his house and were parked on his drive.

Logan switched off the engine and turned to face him.

"You're scaring me, Miles," he said stiffly.

Miles's gut churned with remorse when he saw the concern darkening Logan's beautiful eyes. He unclipped his seat belt, leaned over the console, and kissed Logan.

Logan drew a sharp breath. Then his hands were on Miles's face and his tongue was inside Miles's mouth and Miles forgot all his worries for a dizzying minute.

His pulse was thumping hard when Logan reluctantly ended their kiss.

Logan clasped his face. "What's wrong?"

Miles swallowed and clenched his hands in Logan's shirt. "I—I overheard you and Izzy on the porch."

"Oh." Logan blinked. His mouth twisted in a grimace. "Damn."

"Yeah." A humorless chuckle left Miles. "Damn." He dropped his forehead against Logan's chest. "I don't know what to do. What to think."

Logan wrapped his arms around him. "Are you feeling guilty?"

Miles took a shaky breath. "Yeah."

"Why?"

The question threw Miles. He raised his head and looked blankly at Logan. "What?"

Logan took hold of Miles's chin. "There's no reason for you to feel guilty, Miles. You have no control over Izzy's feelings. She knows that."

"But—" Miles stopped, his insides twisting hotly, "but I wasn't aware she felt that way about me!"

Logan cocked his head to the side. "Would it have changed anything?"

The tumultuous thoughts that had been roaring through Miles's mind ever since he accidentally listened in on Izzy and Logan's private conversation crashed to a halt.

Logan sighed and pressed his lips to Miles's feverish brow. "Would you have reciprocated Izzy's feelings?" he said softly against Miles's skin. He pulled back and gazed intently into Miles's eyes. "Would the two of you have gone out?"

"No," Miles mumbled.

"Then Izzy did the right thing." Logan hugged him tightly. "She has her pride, Miles. Just give her time to work through her feelings and pretend you didn't hear her confession to me."

Miles shuddered and clung to Logan.

Guilt constricted his throat as he listened to the comforting sound of Logan's strong heartbeat. The secret he'd been keeping for the past fifteen years reared its ugly head, mocking him for being a coward.

Miles took a deep breath.

I have to be honest with him. I owe him this much.

"Logan?"

"Yeah?"

"There's—there's something I have to tell you."

Logan tensed a little at his quavering voice.

Miles buried his face in Logan's shirt, his heart pounding so fast he was surprised it hadn't leapt out of his chest.

"I…had a crush on Drake. Before the accident."

His words filled the silence inside the car.

Air whooshed out of Logan. Miles bit his lip.

"Oh, that?" Logan's hands tightened on Miles's back. "Yeah, I guessed that when we were at the bar last week."

Miles froze. He pushed Logan away and stared at him, shocked.

"What? But—how did you—?!"

Logan kissed him.

Miles's thoughts scattered to the four winds. He scowled at Logan when he lifted his mouth off his.

"Stop doing that!" he snapped.

Logan gave him an innocent look. "Stop doing what?"

"Distracting me with your kisses!"

Logan's mouth curved in a lopsided grin. "Did it work?"

Miles punched him lightly in the chest "Yes, it did and I hate you for it," he grumbled.

Logan chuckled. He grabbed Miles's hand and kissed his knuckles. "It wasn't hard to figure out, Miles. The way you look at Drake is different from the way you look at your other friends."

Miles's stomach dropped. "Do you think Drake knows?!" he mumbled, horrified. "And the others?!"

Logan shook his head. "I seriously doubt anyone else is aware you liked Drake that way, least of all Drake." He made a face. "I get the feeling that guy gave his rockstar boyfriend a run for his money before they decided to settle down."

Miles's shoulders sagged. "Thank God!"

"Why did you never confess to Drake?" Logan asked curiously after a moment.

"Oh." Miles blinked. "I guess you wouldn't know. Drake and Alex were going out before the accident."

Logan's eyes widened. "*Get out!* Those two? Really?!"

Miles smiled at his stunned look. "I thought you said you could read people."

Logan rolled his eyes. "I'm not psychic, Miles."

Miles laughed, his chest loosening as the strain he'd been under for most of the night finally melted away. He stiffened when Logan peeled back the sleeve of his jacket and pressed his mouth to his wrist.

Miles shivered. "What are you doing?"

Logan brushed his lips across Miles's quickening

pulse. "Seducing you." He gazed hotly at Miles from under his lashes.

Miles swallowed, his skin prickling with a delicious tension. "What happened to the three-date rule?"

Logan straightened. "Well, technically, if we count our trip to *The Watering Hole* and tonight, we've completed that requirement," he said, deadpan.

Miles stared before snorting. "Man, you have it bad, don't you?"

Logan flashed his teeth. "Guilty as charged."

Miles's breathing quickened as the air between them thickened with sexual tension. Logan's eyes darkened. He leaned in and took Miles's mouth in a kiss that made his toes curl.

"Your place or mine?" Logan whispered against his lips. He arched an eyebrow. "I finished putting my new bedroom furniture together yesterday."

Miles flushed. "Your place."

Logan let Blue and Pepper out of the SUV and took Miles's hand as they crossed the road to his house.

"Just so you know, we're still not going all the way."

A chuckle left him at Miles's disappointed expression.

Miles chewed his lip. "So, what are we going to do?"

He gasped when Logan lifted his hand and sank his teeth into the pulse thrumming at his wrist.

"Things that will make you cry in pleasure," Logan promised with a wicked smile.

Miles's stomach knotted with anticipation.

Logan opened his front door and pulled Miles inside the foyer. The Tiffany lamp burning on the hallway table cast a soft light on Miles's face, making his eyes sparkle.

Logan's cock throbbed painfully at the sight of Miles's flushed cheeks and parted lips.

He wasn't sure how he was going to hold back when all he wanted to do was sink his raging erection inside Miles's body and claim him until he screamed and convulsed in pleasure.

Logan ushered Pepper and Blue into the kitchen and closed the door on the two dogs. Blue whined and scratched the wood for a moment before going quiet.

"He'll be okay," Logan said at Miles's slightly worried look. He held out his hand.

Miles clasped his fingers, his skin hot to the touch.

Blood rushed in Logan's ears as he guided Miles upstairs and across the landing to the master bedroom.

Miles stopped in the middle of the shadowy room and swallowed as he looked around.

Logan crossed the floor, switched on the bedside lamps, and drew the curtains on the windows. He retraced his steps and shut the bedroom door before leaning his back against it.

Miles twisted around and met his heated stare, his erection denting the front of his jeans.

"Come here," Logan said hoarsely.

Miles rushed to him.

Their mouths met in a clash of lips and tongues and teeth, the passion that had burned brightly between them for a week finally exploding.

Miles hummed when Logan nudged his chin up and rained blistering kisses down the column of his throat.

"Fuck!" Logan cursed. "You have no idea how good you taste!"

He bit Miles's skin, grasped his waist, and pulled him close so he could grind their groins together.

Miles clutched Logan's shoulders when Logan rocked and thrust his hips.

"That—I like that!" he gasped.

Logan shivered and straightened so he could stare into Miles's glazed eyes.

Hearing Miles express what he wanted was a world away from the shy young man who'd turned up on the doorstep of his clinic on that stormy day. He wondered if Miles realized what a sexual being he was and how much that fact turned Logan on.

Logan shrugged Miles's jacket off his shoulders and got busy on the rest of his clothes, his mouth finding

Miles's lips again and again. Miles panted as Logan took his shirt off before undoing his belt buckle.

The soft swish of leather and the metallic hiss of Miles's zipper mixed with the sounds of their heavy breathing as their tongues clashed in a heady dance.

Miles shuddered when Logan peeled his jeans and boxers down his legs. He stepped out of them, his erection bobbing against his taut stomach.

Logan caressed his flushed shaft with a knuckle as he straightened.

Miles jerked, his belly contracting.

Logan began undoing the buttons of his shirt, only to freeze when Miles took hold of his hands and shook his head.

"Let me," Miles breathed, his pupils so large Logan could barely see his irises.

Logan kept still by a sheer act of will as Miles slowly unbuttoned his shirt. Miles stared raptly at every inch of skin he exposed, like he was uncovering treasure.

"I love your body," he mumbled. "It's so different from mine."

Logan's muscles jumped as Miles traced his torso and his six-pack with his fingers. Miles bit his lip when his hands found Logan's belt.

Logan closed his fingers atop Miles's and helped him take off the rest of his clothes. He shuddered when Miles touched his naked cock.

A sliver of apprehension clouded Miles's face. "Are you sure this is gonna fit inside me?"

Logan choked on a groan as Miles closed his hand

around his shaft and measured his girth with a doubtful stare.

"It'll fit." He grabbed Miles's hips and backed him across the room to the bed.

Miles's knees struck the edge of the mattress. His breath left him on a surprised whoosh as he tumbled onto the bed.

Logan climbed on and crowded him into the middle.

Miles looked at him feverishly where he loomed above him, his fingers clenching on the sheets.

Logan slowly raked Miles's naked body with his gaze, his heart pounding.

"You're so goddamn beautiful I'm almost scared to touch you, Miles," he said reverently.

Miles shivered, his dick jerking and oozing precum. He grasped Logan's face and pulled him down for a kiss.

"I thought you promised to make me cry with pleasure," he mumbled against Logan's lips.

Logan cursed. He took Miles's wrists and pinned them above his head before lowering his body onto Miles's trembling form.

Miles sucked in air at the full contact.

Logan gnashed his teeth, barely hanging on to his self-control as he settled his weight on Miles and made him sink into the bed.

His every nerve ending was being set ablaze by Miles's skin.

Their cocks brushed, eliciting a sweet sound from Miles.

Logan took his lips passionately. Miles's tongue met his boldly when he swept inside his mouth.

❧

MILES LOST HIMSELF IN THE TORRID KISS, THE electricity sparking through his flesh causing his cock to tingle and throb.

He couldn't believe how good Logan's body felt atop him. He thought it would be suffocating having a man crush him into a bed. The reality couldn't be further from the truth.

Even though he was a virgin, the way Logan pressed into him made him want to be claimed. To be possessed in the most carnal way possible. He wanted Logan to ruin him. To spread him open and plunder his most intimate parts. To dominate him and make him beg for his pleasure.

Miles shuddered at the wanton thoughts storming his mind. A few weeks ago, they would have scared him senseless. Now, all he wanted was to surrender his body and his soul to Logan and let him wreck him any which way he wanted.

He moaned out a protest when Logan wrenched their mouths apart.

Logan tilted Miles's chin up and pressed hot kisses down his throat, his hands trailing sensuously along the underside of Miles's arms. Miles jerked when Logan nipped his skin lightly before sucking the love bite he'd made.

Logan moved down.

Heat flooded Miles's face when his cock left a sticky trail on Logan's belly. The muskiness of his precum mixed with Logan's scent until he was fairly drowning in the intoxicating smell of their sex.

Logan licked the pulse beating wildly at the base of Miles's throat.

"I could get addicted to your taste," he groaned.

Miles cried out when Logan sank his teeth fully into his flesh, to the point he almost broke his skin. The sharp prick of pleasure-pain made Miles's cock pulse and his ass twitch. Logan lapped at the sting and soothed it with soft kisses, his hands skimming Miles's chest.

Miles's breathing accelerated when Logan found his nipples. He closed his eyes and squirmed as Logan twisted and tugged his sensitive nubs with his clever fingers.

"*Ah!*" Miles's eyes slammed open.

Logan had blown out a hot breath on his left nub.

Miles shuddered, his entire body tingling at the sensation. His ass contracted when Logan repeated the motion. Miles flushed and looked down. He bit his lip at the sensual look Logan gave him from under his lashes.

An incoherent sound choked Miles's throat when Logan flicked his stiff flesh with his tongue. Miles's hands found Logan's head, his fingers sinking demandingly into his hair.

"Do you like that?" Logan growled.

Miles's breath caught again and again as Logan circled his nipple with his tongue.

"*Yes!* That feels—*Oh!*"

Logan had closed his mouth on his left breast and was sucking him with powerful contractions of his jaws, his tongue lashing and teasing Miles's nipple in the hot confines of his mouth. His fingers remained busy on Miles's right nub, tugging and pinching so it throbbed with jolts of electrifying pleasure-pain.

Miles moaned and gasped and keened, head thrashing on the pillow. He let go of Logan and clutched the sheets in a white-knuckled grip, his senses overwhelmed by everything Logan was doing to him.

His virgin hole spasmed hungrily, eager for something he had yet to experience. Miles bent his knees and dropped his legs open, obeying his body's instincts to be possessed.

Logan made a savage sound when he sank into the hot cradle of Miles's thighs.

Exquisite tension tightened Miles's spine and belly as Logan took turns worshipping his nipples with his sinful lips and tongue. Surprise had his eyes flaring.

"Logan!"

"Yes, Miles?" Logan flicked his right nipple with his fingers.

"*Ah!* I'm gonna—*I'm gonna come!*"

Miles arched his back and bucked his hips, his entire body tightening like a bow as the first tendrils of his orgasm raced through his nerve endings. He hissed when Logan's hand found his sensitized cock.

Logan started rubbing him briskly.

Miles's moans grew louder as he neared his climax. He thrust his erection shamelessly through Logan's tight grip, seeking a release he knew would blow his mind.

A startled cry left him when Logan closed his teeth on his right nipple and tugged sharply at the same time he rubbed his thumb across the sensitive head of his dick.

The sound turned into a guttural sob when Miles finally crested the dizzying height Logan had brought him to and fell into a valley of blinding pleasure. His belly knotted painfully and his back bowed as he ejaculated all over Logan's hand and belly, his ass spasming with each wave of ecstasy wrecking his senses.

CHAPTER EIGHTEEN

MILES RODE HIS ORGASM FOR WHAT FELT LIKE FOREVER before finally slumping into the bed, his body lax and his mind fuzzy. He blinked sweat out of his eyes and looked blearily at Logan, his chest shuddering with his breaths.

"Was that good?" Logan's eyes were dark and his cheeks flushed with passion as he traced Miles's spent cock with a finger.

Miles shivered. "It was—it was amazing!"

"Good," Logan said. "We're just getting started."

Miles's eyes widened. He swallowed. "We—we are?!"

A wicked smile stretched Logan's mouth. He ducked his head and shifted down the bed so he could kiss Miles's trembling six-pack.

Miles blinked when Logan grabbed a pillow and slipped it under his back. "What—?!"

Logan looked up at him and caressed his shaft. "This will make it easier for both of us."

Miles jerked, arousal stirring at Logan's touch. He gasped when Logan circled his tongue inside his belly button before pressing hot kisses down the thin trail of hair arrowing toward his twitching cock.

His face grew hot when he realized what Logan intended. "Oh."

Logan chuckled at Miles's thrilled expression and the sight of his rapidly swelling dick.

"That's right, Miles. I'm going to eat your pretty cock."

Miles squirmed when Logan closed his hand on his shaft and worked him to a full erection. Then Logan spread his thighs open, hooked his legs over his shoulders, and positioned himself above Miles's trembling member.

Miles's breath froze in his lungs as he watched Logan's wicked tongue dart out and flick his oozing tip. He flinched and shuddered, his heels digging into Logan's back at the spine-tingling sensation. Miles rolled his hips, seeking more of the sinful feeling.

Logan growled when his cock bumped his lips. He opened his mouth and swallowed the head of Miles's erection inside the velvety confines of his cheeks.

"Logan!" Miles's eyes rounded at the pleasure that flooded his body, his shout echoing around the bedroom.

This was like nothing he'd ever experienced before.

Miles panted and looked down his body, his ears buzzing and his skull full of the sound of his pounding heart.

Logan met his wild gaze, wrapped his tongue around his quivering erection, and sucked him deeper.

"Oh God!" Miles cried out. "Logan! *Logan!*"

Logan started bobbing his head up and down, his lips dragging sensuously on Miles's taut flesh while his tongue teased and sucked him.

Logan's name became a breathless chant on Miles's lips as pleasure shot through him again and again, bolts of pure electricity that made his nipples throb and his belly tighten and his hole ache.

The pleasure intensified as Logan worked him expertly, his jaws applying just the right suction to drive Miles out of his mind.

Miles bowed his back and gazed blindly at the ceiling as his body fell into a rhythm as old as time. He danced on the bed, his hips rocking sensuously and thrusting his aching dick in and out of Logan's eager mouth, his hands finding Logan's hair so he could better guide him.

Logan's wicked lips. The silken heat of his cheeks. His masterful tongue. The scalding depths of his tight throat.

Miles's breath hitched as the incredible sensations Logan was giving him began to overwhelm him. He was dimly conscious of Logan smearing the cum covering his belly as he bit his lip to curb his wanton sounds.

The movement of Logan's mouth slowed.

Miles twitched when he traced a slick finger down his trembling taint.

"Logan?" He lifted his head off the pillow and gazed

dazedly down the length of his body at Logan, his chest heaving with his breaths.

Logan held his gaze and rubbed his pucker lightly with the pad of his finger, his cheeks bulging with Miles's erection and his eyes so bright with lust Miles feared his stare would burn him.

Miles moaned, his ass contracting.

Logan repeated the motion again.

Miles shuddered at the illicit sensation and rocked his body against Logan's hand, silently inviting his sinful touch.

Logan groaned at the wanton move.

The reverberations vibrated through Miles's flesh, causing him to hiss.

Logan's head rose and fell on Miles's cock as he resumed blowing him in earnest at the same he rubbed the tight folds protecting his hole.

Miles panted and moaned and cursed, hips undulating helplessly on the bed while he gripped the sheets, the dual stimulation hastening his orgasm. The sweetest tension surged and ebbed through his entire being, heating his blood and drawing lewd sounds from his throat.

Logan took him all the way into the back of his throat and slowly pushed a finger through his softened folds and inside his ass.

The penetration tipped Miles over the edge he'd been surfing.

His mouth opened on a soundless scream and his belly contracting painfully as he curled his body and flexed his toes in midair. His neck corded, his entire body convulsing with a devastating pleasure that seared his senses until he was blind and deaf to everything but the ecstasy drowning him and the jerks of his cock as he spilled his seed inside Logan's throat.

It felt like a lifetime before Miles's awareness returned.

He opened his eyes languidly, his sweat-soaked body limp, his heart beating heavily against his ribs. He sucked in air at the sight that met him.

Logan was kneeling on the bed between his legs and rubbing his turgid erection briskly, his face flushed and his jaw clenched.

"Get on your front, Miles," he ordered gruffly.

Miles swallowed and rolled onto his belly.

He gasped when Logan took hold of his waist and pulled him up on all fours. Logan's next command had Miles biting his lip.

"Spread your legs a little."

Miles did as he was told.

Logan inserted his quivering cock in the gap between Miles's thighs. Miles shuddered when his hot shaft rubbed his sensitive taint. His heart raced as Logan sank his hands into his hips and began thrusting, his precum slicking up the insides of Miles's legs.

Miles rocked to and fro with Logan's powerful motions, his entire being buzzing at the way Logan was using his body to pleasure himself. He flushed when his spent cock stirred.

Logan leaned down and kissed his spine.

"Touch yourself, Miles," he said hoarsely. "Let's come together."

Miles shuddered. He dropped a hand to his pleasantly used member and started rubbing himself.

Logan's breaths grew louder and harsher as he punched his cock between Miles's thighs, kneaded Miles's taint and the underside of his balls.

The bed started to shake with his passionate movements.

Miles hissed when Logan sank his teeth in his shoulder.

"One day," Logan promised roughly. "One day, we'll do this in front of a mirror. I want you to see your face when I take you from the back and sink my cock so deep inside your hole you won't know where my body begins and yours ends!"

Miles's nipples throbbed and his ass twitched hungrily at the torrid image Logan painted. Precum leaked from his swollen shaft and dripped onto the sheet as he worked his flesh briskly.

"*Fuuuccck!*" Logan groaned. "I'm close!"

Miles moaned and accelerated the motion of his hand. His climax spiraled down his spine and tightened his limbs.

Logan stiffened. He came on a guttural shout, his hot seed striking the back of Miles's fingers and his cock in explosive spurts before dripping onto the bed, his hips jackknifing against Miles's ass.

Miles shuddered as his orgasm rolled through him. He ejaculated all over the sheets, his body twitching fitfully and his cock and ass throbbing so hard he thought he would faint.

Logan collapsed on top of him and took him down on the bed.

Miles shivered as Logan's weight crushed him into the mattress and his oozing cock nestled in the valley between his butt cheeks. Their pants filled the bedroom.

Logan's lips ghosted across Miles's nape. "Are you okay?"

Miles swallowed and nodded. "I'm more than okay."

A startled sound left him when Logan flipped him on his back and settled in the cradle of his thighs. Logan tugged Miles's right leg up over his hip and kissed him sweetly.

"That was hands down one of the best sexual experiences I've ever had," he said sultrily against Miles's lips.

Miles's face grew hot at his sensual stare. "It was?"

"Yup." Logan smiled. "I suspect the one I'll have when I'm inside you will be ever better."

Miles's hole spasmed. "When—when will that be?"

Logan chuckled at his eager tone. "Not for a while." He rubbed their noses together. "We need to get you used to my fingers first."

Miles's face fell. "Oh."

Logan laughed. Miles bit his lip when the vibrations echoed through his body.

"We should wash up and change these sheets," Logan said.

Miles swallowed a protest when Logan rose off

him. He'd been relishing the heady feel of Logan's powerful body on his own.

Logan grinned like he'd read his thoughts. "I can literally see the dirty thought you're having right now, Mr. Martinez."

Miles pursed his mouth.

Logan chuckled and pulled him off the bed and into the bathroom.

CHAPTER NINETEEN

Miles woke up to Blue's excited yip. He opened his eyes in time to see the puppy prop his forepaws on the edge of Logan's bed. Blue stretched his neck and licked Miles's nose.

"Hey, Blue," Miles mumbled sleepily. He rolled onto his back and squinted at the sunlight streaming through the gaps in the curtains.

Logan came into the bedroom with two cups of steaming coffee, Pepper padding silently at his side. "Good morning." He smiled at Miles. "It's still early. You should get some more sleep."

Miles's belly clenched.

Logan dressed for work looked good enough to eat.

Logan smirked. "Do you like what you see, Mr. Martinez?"

Heat warmed Miles's cheeks. "I do." He sat up.

The sheets pooled around his waist.

Miles's eyes rounded when he saw the love bites Logan had made all over his body.

"Yikes," Logan muttered, not sounding the least bit sorry. "Looks like I got a bit carried away last night."

Miles took the coffee he offered. "You were like a starving beast," he mumbled.

Logan shrugged, his eyes sparkling with amusement. "What can I say? My prey was just too cute."

Miles groaned. Logan laughed, sat on the bed, and kissed him.

Miles's pulse quickened when he tasted coffee and an essence that was pure Logan. He hummed appreciatively.

Logan reluctantly ended the kiss. "What are your plans for the day?"

Miles bent his knees and cradled his cup in his hands. "I'm going to apply for college."

Logan's eyes widened. "What?"

Miles leaned over and pressed a quick peck to Logan's mouth, unable to resist touching the man who'd wormed his way into his heart and soul.

"I've always wanted to be a PE teacher," Miles confessed. "I've been looking at an education major the last few weeks. I ordered some brochures, but they've been sitting unopened in a drawer." He took a deep breath and met Logan's surprised gaze unflinchingly, his chest tight with all the wonderful and scary emotions Logan had roused in him in the past few weeks. "Meeting you was what I needed to start moving forward again. To...live again." He tugged his bottom lip between his teeth, feeling shy all of a sudden.

Admiration brightened Logan's eyes. He reached over and brushed a thumb across Miles's mouth so he released his trapped lip.

"That's incredible, Miles. I'm so proud of you."

Miles blushed.

Logan put their cups on the nightstand, clasped Miles's face, and took his mouth in a soul-searing kiss.

By the time they came up for air, they were both flushed and breathless.

Logan pressed his forehead against Miles's brow and groaned. "If I didn't have surgery this morning, I'd definitely skip work and climb back in that bed with you."

Miles chuckled. "I can't corrupt Twilight Falls' hottest vet."

Logan raised an eyebrow. "You think I'm hot?"

"Ah-huh." Miles shocked both of them when he lowered his hand and grazed Logan's erection. "And incredibly well endowed."

Logan cursed. Miles grinned.

Logan rose. "I have to go," he said wistfully.

Miles folded his arms atop his knees. "Have a great day."

Logan's expression turned complicated.

"What?" Miles said, puzzled.

"You have no idea how delectable you look right now," Logan said heatedly. "Maybe I should cancel that surgery after all."

Miles laughed, his heart swelling with happiness. "Go!"

"I'll make dinner tonight," Logan promised as he walked out the bedroom.

"I'll see you later."

Miles listened to the sound of the front door closing and Logan's pickup driving off. He buried his face in his hands, unable to stop the goofy smile stretching his mouth.

He'd thought things might be awkward between them after last night. Instead, sharing a morning with Logan felt as natural as breathing.

Blue whined. Miles raised his head.

The puppy glanced at him before padding to the bedroom door, his tail drooping.

"It's okay, Blue. Pepper will be back soon." Miles climbed out of bed. "Wanna go for a run?"

Blue's ears perked up. He yipped, his tail swinging excitedly.

Miles got dressed and was halfway down the stairs when an idea came to him. He hesitated before taking his cell out of his pocket. He sent a text to Elijah before he could change his mind. Elijah replied right away.

It was mid-morning when Miles opened the back door of *La Petite Bouche Gourmande* and walked into Elijah's bakery.

Elijah greeted him with a smile where he was measuring flour into a bowl at one of the counters. "Hey. Why don't you take a seat? I'll be finished with this batch soon."

Miles slowed when he saw the two men seated at the kitchen island. "What are you guys doing here?"

Alex shrugged. "We came for breakfast."

"Same," Hunter added shamelessly, indicating his coffee and blueberry muffin.

Elijah chuckled at Miles's mildly disapproving look. "It's alright. I like it when you guys keep me company."

The rear door squeaked open. Roman tumbled in with a haggard expression, his hair askew.

"Elijah," the rockstar moaned. He staggered over the chef and dropped his head on his shoulder. "I need coffee and croissants."

Elijah patted his back with an indulgent expression. "Is the new song still giving you trouble?"

"Yeah." Roman sighed and looped his arms around Elijah's waist. "I keep messing up the lyrics. All I can think about is my wedding with Drake." He rubbed his nose in Elijah's chef uniform. "You smell nice."

"Carter would have a heart attack if he saw you two right now," Alex told Elijah drily.

"Never mind Carter," Hunter muttered. "Drake would be foaming at the mouth."

The swing door to the eatery opened, bringing with it the sound of the morning crowd packing the shop. Sam Harris, Elijah's bakery manager, poked her head through the gap.

"I heard voices." Her eyes narrowed when she saw Roman. "How about you stop clinging to my boss and let him work? There's a line of people out here waiting for his baked goods."

"You know, you used to show me a lot more respect when we first met," Roman grumbled.

"That's before I got to know the real you, Sloth

Boy," Sam grunted. Her expression softened at the sight of Miles. "Want your usual?"

Miles smiled and nodded.

"Ah." Sam's face grew misty. "If only I was into dicks. I'd definitely try and seduce you." She disappeared.

Miles's ears grew warm.

Roman sniffed. "That's preferential treatment, that is."

Nathan came in through the back door. "You got something extra sweet I can feed Wyatt?" he asked Elijah distractedly. "He's like a bear with a sore head."

Hunter grimaced. "That time of the month, huh?"

Nathan's expression grew pinched. "Don't even joke about it. We've got a deadline coming up, so we haven't had sex in a week. I didn't know his withdrawal symptoms would get this bad."

"Wow," Roman mumbled. "And I thought I had problems."

"Why don't you guys have a quickie at the office?" Hunter shrugged. "I do it all the time with Theo." He winked and gave them a thumbs up. "It's the best."

Nathan grimaced. Elijah sighed.

"You're despicable," Alex told Hunter leadenly.

"I'm never sitting on Theo's office couch again," Roman vowed.

Miles waited until Sam had brought his coffee through and left before leaning against the counter beside Elijah and eyeing the four men in the kitchen.

Might as well as all of them.

He took a deep breath. "Can you guys teach me how to bottom?"

Elijah accidentally crushed the egg he'd been about to break into the mixing bowl. Hunter choked on his muffin. Alex spat out his coffee. Nathan dropped the eclair he'd been about to bite into. Roman's jaw sagged open.

"You mean—" Hunter gulped, "like—group sex?!"

Roman closed his mouth and dinged Hunter on the back of his head. "No, he doesn't, you dirt bag!" he hissed.

Nathan shook his head pityingly at Hunter. "Dude."

"I'm getting a sense of déjà vu," Alex mumbled.

Elijah cleaned his hands at the sink and dried them on a towel. "Is this about Logan?"

"Yeah." Miles rubbed the back of his neck and made a face. "We…kinda had sex last night. But we didn't go all the way. Logan says he wants to take things slow."

Alex arched an eyebrow. "And you don't?"

"I told Logan I wanted him to ruin me, but he said that my virginity was too precious and that we'd have penetrative sex when I get used to his fingers." Miles sighed. "But he's only put the one inside me so far. At this rate, it'll take forever before I get my cherry popped."

Elijah bit his lip hard, his shoulders trembling as he choked back laughter. The others groaned.

"You know, those words and your face don't match," Nathan mumbled.

"Agreed," Roman muttered. "It's like hearing Bambi say he wants to be eaten by a wolf."

Miles rolled his eyes.

Hunter propped his elbows on the breakfast bar and watched Miles thoughtfully.

"Few people know this, but Theo is only the second man I've ever bottomed for," he said in a serious tone Miles had rarely heard. "He's the one who taught me how to enjoy that role. I was worried at first as I'd been an exclusive top before that, but we took our time and did a few things to get my body ready."

Miles's pulse quickened. "What did you do?"

Hunter smiled faintly. "We used toys. I can recommend some."

Five days later found Miles sitting on his bed and staring at the contents of the box he'd just taken delivery of. He swallowed.

It contained an array of sex toys and love beads in discreet packaging.

"I don't even know what half of these are," Miles mumbled to Blue.

Blue jumped on the bed and sniffed the box. He sneezed on some packing foam.

Miles glanced at the clock. Logan wouldn't be home for at least another couple of hours.

Determination tightened Miles's jaw. He shut Blue in the kitchen with his play things and some doggie treats and went upstairs to his bedroom.

Miles took a bottle of peach-scented lube out of the box and eyed the black, anal dildo Hunter had recommended he start with. A shiver that was half apprehension, half anticipation raised goosebumps on his skin. He removed the toy from its package and went into the shower to prep his body like Elijah and the others had explained.

By the time he finished cleaning and stimulating his most intimate part, Miles was sporting an erection and the tight folds guarding his passage had softened enough for him to slip a finger inside himself.

His face warmed as he explored his entrance and his tingling nerve endings.

I think I'm ready.

※

LOGAN PULLED UP ON HIS DRIVEWAY AND SWITCHED OFF the engine of the pickup. He'd had a couple of last minute cancellations and had ended up finishing earlier than he'd thought he would. He let Pepper out and looked over at Miles's house.

Miles's SUV was parked on his drive.

Logan hesitated. They'd made plans to go out for dinner that night.

I should give him some alone time before I go over.

Logan was halfway to his front door when he whirled around and headed resolutely across the road. He wanted to see Miles. A grimace twisted his mouth.

Let's face it, I want to do more than just see him.

The memory of how Miles had looked when he'd shattered in his arms that morning had Logan's cock twitching. They'd slept with each other every day since that first time on poker night. Logan had relished discovering all the ways he could drive Miles out of his mind with pleasure since then, including fingering his ass. But it wasn't just Miles who'd experienced some spectacular orgasms.

Miles had been keen to learn how to blow him and Logan had finally guided him through the act last week. A vision of Miles kneeling on the edge of his bed last night and hungrily swallowing his cock as he stood above him flashed before Logan's eyes. He bit back a groan.

Yeah, that's a mental picture I'll definitely be taking to my grave.

Logan used the spare key Miles had given him and let himself inside the house.

"Miles?" he called out.

A yip came from the kitchen. Logan went over, opened the door, and was almost bowled over by Blue. Blue jumped up and licked his chin enthusiastically as he leaned down to scratch his head. The puppy greeted Pepper with an excited sound.

Logan left the dogs in the kitchen and went in search of Miles. He'd cleared the downstairs and was approaching Miles's bedroom on the second floor when a low sound reached him. He slowed.

The sound came again. It was Miles moaning.

Logan's pulse quickened with alarm. He rushed to the door and opened it, only to freeze in his tracks.

Miles was naked on his bed. He was kneeling and gripping the headboard with a white-knuckled fist while he worked his ass open with a thin dildo, his erection bobbing against his stomach.

Logan's breath caught at the erotic sight.

Miles startled when he heard Logan's low gasp. He

straightened and removed the love toy from his body, an embarrassed flush creeping up his chest and cheeks.

"You should have kept it in," Logan blurted out before he could stop himself.

Miles blinked.

Logan came inside the bedroom and closed the door. His foot struck a box as he started across the floor. He stopped and looked down.

It was full of sex toys.

Logan shivered, lust instantly heating up his blood.

"Miles, is there something you want to tell me?" He tugged slowly at the knot in his tie and slipped it from around his neck, his pulse accelerating.

Miles's pupils dilated when Logan shrugged out of his jacket and started unbuttoning his shirt.

"You haven't answered my question." Logan kicked off his socks and shoes and started on his belt buckle, his heart slamming against his ribs and his gaze burning into the blushing face of the naked man on the bed.

"I—I asked some of guys about bottoming last week." Miles swallowed before jutting his chin, his expression defiant. "I wanted to learn how I could get my body ready for you."

Logan's hands stilled on his zipper. "And they suggested you try these toys?"

Miles nodded.

Logan's belly clenched. *He's gonna make me lose my mind.*

"Is that the first one you've used?" He indicated the dildo in Miles's hand with a jerk of his head.

"Yeah." Miles chewed his bottom lip. "They told me to prep myself so I had a long shower first."

Logan removed the rest of his clothes, eyed the contents of the box, and selected some anal beads.

Miles's eyes widened at the sight of Logan's engorged cock and the toys in his hands. "Hmm, Logan?" He licked his lips, hope brightening his eyes.

"These will make it easier to stimulate your sweet spot." Logan took the beads out of their packaging and made his way to the bed. "But first things first."

He climbed on, pushed Miles onto his back, and straddled his body.

"You've been a bad, bad boy, Miles Martinez," Logan said sternly. "Now, get ready to be punished."

Miles shivered as Logan pushed his arms above his head. His mouth parted on a soft gasp when Logan looped his tie around his wrists and secured the end to the central bed post.

Miles's cock jerked out a shot of precum. His breathing quickened, his excitement clear as day.

Blood pounded in Logan's veins at the delicious sight of Miles all tied up and eager and pliant before him. Miles had a way of bringing out a side of him he hadn't even known he possessed. One that was savage with a need to own and to subjugate.

He pushed a pillow under Miles's lower back, took the open bottle of lube on the beside table, and liberally coated his hand and the dildo Miles had been playing with.

"How far in did you go with this?" Logan asked between clenched teeth.

Miles shuddered. "A—about a third of the way."

His eyes rounded when Logan lifted his calves onto his shoulders. Logan leaned down and flicked the head of Miles's cock with his tongue.

Miles cried out and bucked his hips.

"And how did it feel?" Logan swirled his tongue around Miles's slit and fondled his balls.

"*Ah!*" Miles spread his thighs wide, offering Logan a dizzying view of his taint and the twitching folds of his glistening pucker. "It felt—it felt good!"

Logan let go of Miles's shaft and rubbed his hole with his thumb. He hissed when it gave away slickly, allowing him to slip inside. He removed his finger, pressed the tip of the dildo to Miles's hungry entrance, and pushed in.

A buzzing noise filled his ears when Miles's body opened up and accepted the stiff intruder.

"Shit," Logan groaned. "This is the hottest thing I've ever seen in my life!"

Miles moaned as Logan worked the toy inside him with gentle thrusts and twists. He stiffened when it reached the inner ring of muscles guarding his passage.

Logan took hold of Miles's dick with his slicked up fingers and started stroking him, his own erection throbbing painfully between his thighs.

Miles tugged his lower lip between his teeth and grunted and moaned at the dual stimulation. His hips began undulating with a sensuousness that made Logan swallow a curse.

"Breathe in and out through your nose, Miles,"

Logan grated as he pressed the dildo firmly against the tightest part of Miles's passage.

Miles panted and did as Logan ordered. His body slowly relaxed.

Logan circled the head of Miles's cock with his thumb.

Miles's stomach contracted and his ass pulsed around the toy.

Logan pushed it through the spasming band.

CHAPTER TWENTY-ONE

"OH!" MILES'S EYES ROUNDED AS THE TOY BREACHED THE tight ring and filled him up. He panted and looked dazedly at Logan. "Is it in?!"

"Yeah." Logan pulled the toy out halfway and pushed it back in.

"*Oh!*" Miles's knuckles whitened around the tie. His hips jerked.

Logan gave in to his instincts, leaned down to swallow Miles's cock, and began working his front and back end at the same time. Miles panted and gasped sultrily as Logan blew him and stretched him open.

A protest left him when Logan released his dick and removed the dildo.

Logan lubed up the first set of love beads and pressed the smallest sphere inside Miles, his mouth dry. He cursed at the hungry way Miles's ass swallowed it.

Shit. Will he take my dick as easily?!

Miles hummed as Logan worked the toy inside him.

Logan knew he'd found his prostate when he suddenly stiffened and cried out.

Miles looked numbly at Logan. "What—what was that?!"

"That was your sweet spot, Miles." Logan kissed the inside of his thigh, worked the toy all the way inside him, and slowly pulled it out.

Miles's eyes rolled back into his head as the beads massaged his prostate one by one. He punched his hips off the pillow, his heels digging into Logan's back and his belly contracting so hard he winced.

Logan's breaths came in shuddering pants as he watched him.

Miles collapsed down a moment later, his face slick with sweat and his body trembling.

"That was a dry orgasm, Miles," Logan said hoarsely.

He stretched Miles's passage with the toy before extracting it from his ass.

Miles whimpered, his hole spasming.

Logan took the next set of beads. They were bigger than the first ones.

Miles's lips parted as he watched Logan prep the toy with plenty of lube, his eyes so dark with lustful anticipation Logan almost gave in to his animal instinct to take him there and then.

Logan resisted the urge to stroke his own cock as he stretched Miles's loose pucker with his thumb and pushed the first bead in. Miles gasped at the girth of the spheres slowly penetrating his body. His low hum and the way he squeezed his hole told

Logan he was enjoying the filthy sensation of being filled up.

Miles jerked and shuddered as Logan slowly worked the toy in and out of his body, the wicked pops the beads made when they exited his twitching pucker making him gasp over and over again.

Logan gritted his teeth and relentlessly stimulated Miles's prostate, thrilled to be teaching him the hidden pleasures of his body.

Though it was the first time he was using sex toys on a man, he'd read enough about gay sex to get an idea of how they worked. His one visit to a gay sex club in Sacramento had been especially eye-opening and he'd watched in open fascination as the performers on stage indulged in various toys and contraptions to give themselves anal orgasms.

The way Miles was thoroughly relishing his first experience with the sex toys his friends had recommended told Logan this wouldn't be the last time they would be using them in bed.

It's not just him. Logan swallowed. *I could come just watching the way he reacts when I play with his ass.*

"Your body looks like it's loving this, Miles," he growled.

"Ah! *Yes!* Right *there!*" Miles groaned when he twisted the beads. "So good! It feels so good, Logan! Don't stop!" His chest and face reddened and his eyes glazed over as he skirted the edge of his next orgasm.

Logan closed a hand around Miles's cock and began stroking him.

Miles hissed.

Logan pulled the anal beads out, pushed them back all the way in, and began withdrawing the spheres one torturous inch at a time as he rubbed Miles's quivering erection briskly.

Incoherent sounds tumbled from Miles's lips as pleasure overwhelmed him. He rolled his hips and twisted his head so he could bite down on the underside of his arm.

Logan's heart thundered savagely against his ribs. He could tell from the way Miles's stomach was spasming that he was close to climaxing. He released Miles's shaft, pressed the heel of his palm low down on his abdomen, and swallowed his cock with his lips, his hand busy working the love beads out of his tight ass.

A guttural shout left Miles. His eyes rounded and his entire body went rigid.

He bowed his spine and convulsed with sweet violence, his wrists stretching the tie holding him prisoner so taut it almost tore.

Blood rushed in Logan's ears as he gulped the hot seed filling his mouth and throat. He removed the anal beads from Miles's hole and pushed two fingers through his pucker.

They went in easily.

Logan cursed around Miles's cock when Miles's hot passage pulsed and gripped him tightly in the throes of his devastating orgasm.

Miles finally sagged onto the bed, his lip swollen where he'd bitten it, his body twitching with aftershocks of pleasure. He blinked his eyes open when

Logan let go of his spent cock and removed his fingers from his ass.

Logan reached up and undid the tie from around his wrists. He kissed the faint marks they'd left and met Miles's sated stare.

"Was that good?"

Miles nodded numbly. His lips parted when he saw Logan's erection.

"I want to suck you."

Logan's stomach knotted when Miles shifted on all fours. He straightened up on his knees and stroked a thumb across Miles's mouth before slipping it inside.

Miles watched him from under his lashes and sucked on his finger.

Logan's desire reached fever point at his carnal stare.

"Fuck!" He guided his raging member to Miles's eager mouth and pushed it through his full lips.

His eyes almost rolled back in his head at the incredible sensation.

Miles took hold of Logan's hips and worked his tongue around his aching girth, his face flushed with the sinful pleasure of the act. Logan groaned when Miles widened his jaws and took him in deep.

"Miles," Logan mumbled. His entire body pricked and tingled at the wicked sensation of Miles's lips and tongue around his cock. He sank his hands in Miles's hair, pulled out of his mouth, and punched back in with a hiss.

Miles grunted and panted through his nose. He

bobbed his head to and fro, matching Logan's thrusts, his tongue and lips busy on Logan's turgid flesh.

Logan's head fell back. He closed his eyes and lost himself in the moment, his buttocks contracting and relaxing with every roll of his hips, his fingers clenching in Miles's hair. His breathing grew heavier and harsher as his orgasm sparked down his spine and pooled in his belly.

Logan bit his lip and groaned when his cock hit the velvety depths of Miles's throat. His thrusts accelerated, his grip turning punishing as he chased his pleasure. Miles's low moans and the way his fingers twitched on Logan's skin told him he was enjoying the savage way Logan was fucking his mouth.

Logan crested the wave of his climax on a loud curse. He plunged his cock hard and deep inside Miles as he ejaculated with a force that made him dizzy.

Miles swallowed and gulped his cum greedily.

Logan's thrusts slowed as he emptied his jerking dick inside Miles's mouth. The last waves of his climax finally ebbed away, leaving him shuddering and twitching.

Sweat dripped down Logan's face. He removed his spent cock from Miles's lips and gazed at him. Miles's expression made him groan.

He had the look of someone who'd just feasted on the best dish in the whole world.

"That was great," Miles mumbled.

Logan clutched his shoulders and took him down on the bed. They settled on their sides facing one another, their chests heaving while they gazed wondrously into each other's eyes.

"Which part?" Logan grazed Miles's swollen lips with his hand.

Miles kissed his fingers. "All of it." He reached between their bodies and stroked Logan's sensitive cock.

Logan hissed, his flesh tingling.

"But I especially love it when you lose control," Miles confessed breathlessly. "When you fuck me like you can't stop."

Logan cursed, wrapped his arms around Miles, and rolled onto his back.

Miles sucked in air as he found himself atop him.

"How about we rest for a bit and then go again?" Logan looked at the clock on the bedside table. "We still have a couple of hours before our dinner reservation." He smiled seductively, skimmed his hands down Miles's back, and explored his softened pucker with his fingers. "There are a prostate massager and a vibrator in that box I want to try on you."

Miles shivered and nodded.

CHAPTER TWENTY-TWO

Surprise widened Drake's eyes.

"You've applied for college?" Wyatt repeated where they sat at a table at the back of *La Petite Bouche Gourmande*, his expression equally astonished.

"Ah-huh." Miles sipped his coffee. "I'm hoping to get into an education major and train to be a PE teacher."

"You mentioned it once when we were still in high school," Tristan observed. "I didn't think you were serious."

"I am."

Drake leaned back in his chair. A faint smile curved his mouth. "That's great. I'm glad you've decided what you want to do."

Miles's chest loosened. He could read the genuine happiness in Drake's eyes.

This time, his heart did not ache as he gazed at the man he used to love.

The bell above the door tinkled when it opened, bringing with it a gust of cold. Hunter, Nathan, and

Alex piled inside the cake shop. They ordered drinks at the serving counter and made their way over to the table.

"You popped that cherry yet, Martinez?" Hunter said breezily as he took the seat beside Drake.

Heads turned close by. Sam looked over her shoulder where she was working the coffee machine behind the serving counter and narrowed her eyes at them.

Miles sank into his chair with a groan. "How about you not talk about my sex life in public?"

Hunter arched an eyebrow. "That's a no, huh?"

Drake made a face. "You guys still haven't had sex?"

"Keep it down, will you?!" Miles hissed, flushing.

"Man, that Logan has the patience of a saint," Nathan observed.

"It's not that we haven't, you know—done stuff," Miles protested.

Someone choked at the next table.

Sam scowled and stuck her head through the kitchen swing door. "Elijah! Your friends are being perverts again!" she hissed.

Elijah's resigned voice came in the distance. "Let it go, Sam. They were born perverts."

"Hey, I resent that!" Hunter objected. He waited until Sam had gone back to making coffee before leaning closer to Miles. "Did you get the toys I told you about?" He waggled his eyebrows.

"What toys?" Wyatt said, nonplussed.

Nathan grinned. "Hunter told him to get some for ass play."

A cup crashed two tables over.

Tristan groaned. Drake frowned.

The Christmas music playing in the background swelled in volume. Sam glared at them, her hand on the controls of the entertainment system behind the counter.

"I think she wants us to shut up," Miles said guiltily.

Wyatt cocked his head at Nathan. "Want me to buy some?"

Nathan blinked. "Buy some what?"

"Sex toys." Wyatt shrugged. "You look like you wanted to try them."

Nathan's expression glazed over.

Wyatt smiled. "I'll take that as a yes."

"I can give you my list of recs," Hunter said with a smirk.

The conversation soon turned to Christmas. With the weekend festivities only a few days away, they'd started planning what to take to Alex and Finn's place. Elijah and Wyatt were making Christmas lunch and everyone was bringing food and drinks for Christmas Eve.

The sun was sinking behind the mountains when Miles got home. He took Blue out for a walk and returned in time to see Logan pull up on his driveway.

Logan got out of the pickup and grabbed two take out bags from the passenger seat. "I got your favorite, Chinese."

Miles went over and kissed him. "Did you have a good day?"

Logan smiled. "I did, thank you. What did you do?"

They chatted as they went inside Logan's house, the conversation light and easy. Miles got Blue and Pepper dinner while Logan went upstairs to freshen up. He plated their food and grabbed two bottles of beer from the refrigerator before taking the tray into Logan's newly furnished den.

Miles crossed the cozy room and started a fire in the hearth. They'd gotten into the habit of having dinner there, the only light coming from the flames and the soft lamps dotting the side tables and floor.

Not just dinner.

Miles's ears warmed as he looked at the couch. He and Logan had done plenty of other things in his den.

Logan joined him on said couch a moment later. They talked while they ate and finished their beers. Logan sighed and dropped his head against the back rest when Miles returned from clearing the dishes. He wrapped an arm around him and hugged him close.

"I'm really looking forward to the holidays."

"Me too." Miles dropped his head on Logan's shoulder.

"I don't have to go in until lunchtime tomorrow. Want to get some shopping done for the party?"

"That'd be great," Miles replied.

A soft chuckle escaped Logan. Miles looked at him quizzically.

"I was just thinking we're already acting like an old, married couple," Logan said with a grin.

Miles's heart clenched.

"I kinda like the sound of that," he mumbled before he could stop himself.

Logan stilled. His eyes darkened to a stormy slate as he watched Miles. He tipped Miles's chin up with a knuckle and pressed a soft kiss to his mouth.

"I like the sound of that too, Mr. Martinez."

Miles sank into Logan as Logan deepened their kiss. The passion that always simmered under their skin blossomed into a desire that seared their senses. Miles straddled Logan's lap, his erection denting his jeans, sparks exploding in his mouth as they mated their tongues with wild abandon. He gasped when Logan grabbed his thighs and locked them around his hips as he pushed up to his feet.

He carried Miles upstairs, color staining his cheekbones and his erection nudging Miles's stiff dick, his half-lidded gaze burning into Miles as he claimed his mouth.

Miles's breath whooshed out of him when Logan dropped him on his bed. He sat up, peeled his T-shirt off, and kicked off his boxers and jeans while Logan undressed. Logan gave his swollen shaft a few tugs as he climbed on the mattress, his stare predatory.

"Logan?"

"Yeah?" Logan leaned in and kissed the pulse beating frantically at the base of Miles's throat.

Miles shivered and moaned, his head tilting to give him better access. "No toys tonight. I want you."

Logan froze. He lifted his head and met Miles's gaze. "Are you sure?"

Miles nodded.

Logan shuddered. "Okay."

Miles's belly clenched when he reached over and

took condoms and lube out of the bedside drawer. He dropped them on the bed, sat on his knees, and tugged Miles onto his lap.

Miles looped his arms around Logan's neck and met his hungry lips, their cocks brushing. Logan rained kisses down Miles's throat and worshipped his nipples with his fingers and mouth, making him twitch and drawing lustful sounds from his throat. He caressed Miles's trembling stomach and his thighs before teasing his erection with featherlight strokes that made Miles curse.

CHAPTER TWENTY-THREE

Blood pounded inside Miles's skull when Logan lubed his fingers. He dipped his hand under Miles's taint to his pucker. Miles shivered and dropped his head on Logan's shoulder as Logan rubbed and circled his folds.

"Ah!" Miles's hands tightened on Logan's back.

Logan had pushed two fingers inside his ass.

His hole tingled and twitched pleasurably at the sensation of being stretched.

Logan kissed the side of his neck and started plunging his fingers in and out of Miles.

"Fuck!" he growled against his skin. "You're so hot and tight! I can't wait to get inside you!"

"Oh God!" Miles's eyes rolled back in his head when Logan pushed a third finger through his hungry hole. "*Yes!* I want that too!"

He clasped Logan's face and kissed him wildly while Logan plundered his most intimate part. A savage sound left Logan a moment later. He removed his fingers from Miles's throbbing passage, rolled a condom on his straining dick, and poured a generous amount of lube on the rubber.

Miles's breath hitched when Logan gripped his waist and pulled him up on his knees.

"Spread your thighs and take me in, Miles." He kissed Miles's chest and looked at him, his pupils dilated and his irises so dark with lust Miles could only tremble.

Logan snaked his hands around Miles's backside and stretched him open. Miles's heart raced like a freight train as he took hold of Logan's cock from behind, widened his knees, and positioned his slicked up hole so it was lined up with Logan's rigid shaft. His breaths came in heavy pants as he slowly pushed down.

They both cursed when his pucker greedily swallowed the tip of Logan's engorged member.

Logan rolled his hips and nudged his dick in an inch deeper.

Miles hissed when he reached the tightest part of him. He inhaled and exhaled shallowly, forcing his body to relax.

"Look at me," Logan whispered.

Miles met Logan's heated gaze and swallowed. Logan closed his hand on Miles's cock and began lightly stroking him. Miles's breathing accelerated, pleasure coiling through him with every motion of Logan's fingers and the heady feel of Logan's cock inside him. His ass spasmed.

"Bear down, Miles," Logan ordered gruffly. He

grasped Miles's hip and thrust up at the same time Miles sank onto his cock.

Miles's eyes rounded as Logan punched through the taut band of muscles and rammed home. "*Oh!*"

He squeezed his eyes shut and bit his lip at the exquisite sting and burn throbbing through his passage. Logan kept still and pressed soft kisses to his eyelids and face while his body adapted to the penetration.

Miles's heart thundered against his ribs. He couldn't believe how full he felt. Or how crazy good it was to have Logan's dick inside him. He blinked his eyes open and gazed dazedly at Logan.

"You okay?" Logan asked tensely.

Miles nodded. "We should have done this sooner."

Logan groaned. Miles moaned when the reverberations traveled through to his ass. Logan grabbed his hips, withdrew his dick, and punched back in.

Miles cried out at the heady sensation of being impaled, his ass and cock tingling and throbbing. He grabbed onto Logan's shoulders and followed the rhythm he set, bearing down as he pushed up and rolling up as he pulled out.

Miles's toes curled and his head fell back as he and Logan made love, his dick leaving a sticky trail of precum all over Logan's taut belly, bolts of electricity shooting through his entire body.

"So good!" he moaned. "This feels *so good*, Logan!"

Logan growled, looped an arm around his waist, and pushed him down on the bed.

Miles's eyes rounded when the new angle had Logan's plunging cock rubbing his prostate. He bowed his spine on a guttural cry, sparks of pleasure exploding behind his eyelids as he squeezed them shut.

A feral sound left Logan as Miles's ass squeezed and milked his cock. He slipped a pillow under Miles's back, grabbed Miles's calves, and pushed his legs up in the air. Miles blinked dazedly.

Logan held Miles's stunned stare as he propped his shoulders behind his knees, opening him wide.

"You'll like this position too." Logan kissed his thigh, pressed his hands on the mattress on either side of Miles's torso, and pulled his cock out of his hole.

Miles shouted out when he thrust back in and hit his prostate head on.

His fingers found Logan's arms. He held on to him tightly as pleasure throbbed his passage with every thrust, causing his stomach to clench so hard it ached.

"*Ah!* Oh! *Yes!*" Miles chanted breathlessly. "More!"

Logan cursed and gnashed his teeth as he punched his hips against Miles's ass and pierced him with his steely cock.

Tension stiffened Miles's body and pooled in his dick and belly. He came on a sob of pure ecstasy, his shaft pulsing cum all over his stomach.

Logan groaned at the sight. He reached down, took hold of Miles's cock, and rubbed him to a fresh erection.

Miles lost himself to the pleasure of being taken. His whole world focused on Logan's hungry eyes and his corded neck and the way his flushed body undulated as he claimed him with savage passion.

He came one more time before Logan finally neared his climax.

Miles's heart swelled as he watched Logan go rigid and his mouth open on an animal shout. Logan's cock throbbed deep inside him as he convulsed and rammed his hips fitfully against Miles's ass. Logan closed his eyes and dropped his head back, riding the violent waves of his orgasm with shuddering gasps and groans.

His hand grew rough on Miles's trembling cock, hastening his climax.

Miles exploded on Logan's fingers a moment later, his breath hitching repeatedly and his stomach throbbing from the powerful contractions that had wrecked his body.

Logan cursed when Miles's passage kneaded his pulsing dick.

Miles's ears buzzed as he finally came down from the dizzying heights of ecstasy Logan had pushed him to. He looked fuzzily at Logan when he lowered his legs from his shoulders.

Logan wrapped Miles's thighs around his hips and collapsed on top of him.

"That," he panted, "was incredible!"

He raised his head and planted a loving kiss on Miles's mouth, his eyes bright.

Miles licked the drop of sweat on Logan's chin. "Told you we should have done this before."

He moaned a protest when Logan pulled out of his body and discarded the condom.

"You say that now but wait until tomorrow, Mr. Martinez," Logan murmured huskily. He reached down and teased Miles's pleasantly used pucker with his fingers, making him hiss. "You may very well regret those words."

"I won't." Miles's grabbed his errant hand and pressed it firmly to his ass. "This is all your territory now, Mr. Prescott." He smiled seductively. "You can do with it as you please."

Logan blinked before dropping his head on Miles's shoulder with a groan.

"I've created a monster," he mumbled.

Miles laughed, his chest almost bursting with the happiness flooding his heart and soul.

CHAPTER TWENTY-FOUR

CHRISTMAS EVE DAWNED CLEAR AND BRIGHT. LOGAN finished his morning clinic and headed to Alex and Finn's home with Miles in the afternoon.

Snowflakes started spiraling out the sky as he guided his pickup into the shallow, forested valley where Finn's mansion perched on a shallow bluff overlooking a creek.

Logan observed the building's clean lines of the modern building. "This is nice."

"Carter and Elijah got married here." Miles's voice grew melancholic. "Finn had this built when his wife was still alive."

Logan gave him a surprised glance. "Finn was married before he met Alex?"

Miles nodded. "She died of cancer a few years ago."

Several vehicles were already parked in the forecourt in front of the mansion.

Blue yipped excitedly and jumped out of the back of the pickup with Pepper. Logan and Miles let the dogs explore the edge of the forest before getting their overnight bags and the gifts and food they'd brought out of the pickup.

Finn opened the front door just as Miles raised his hand to ring the bell.

"I thought I heard the dogs." He smiled and ushered them inside. Blue and Pepper scampered over and followed.

Logan looked around curiously as they crossed a vestibule with a glass roof. It branched to the west and east wings of the mansion before opening out into an airy space that took about half the width of the building. A floor-to-glass ceiling made up the back wall of the open-plan living and dining room.

It offered breathtaking views over the terrace and the pine forest rising beyond the creek.

A giant Christmas tree decked with lights and baubles dominated the left side of the room. Flames crackled in an open hearth ringed with a fireguard in the middle.

Tristan was drinking coffee on one of the couches. James sat with his legs on Tristan's lap and talked quietly on the phone. He smiled and waved a hand at them.

Maisie looked up where she was coloring a picture book at the coffee table. She beamed. "Blue! Pepper!" She jumped to her feet as the dogs dashed over to greet her, their tails wagging a fast beat.

"Where's everyone?" Miles asked curiously while Finn took their coats.

"Carter only got back from his shoot yesterday so

I'm pretty certain he's molesting his husband in their bedroom," Finn said drily. "Drake and Roman aren't here yet. Izzy and the rest of the guys are in the kitchen."

Alex came down a curved, glass and steel staircase. "I'm glad you put Carter and Elijah at the end of the corridor," he told Finn with a frown. "Let's hope they'll abstain from full on debauchery this weekend."

Tristan narrowed his eyes and indicated Maisie with a sharp tilt of his head.

"What's debau—cherry?" Maisie asked curiously.

Tristan sighed.

"It means your daddies are sharing lots of smoochies," Alex told Maisie without batting an eyelid.

"Babe," Finn mumbled.

"Oh." Maisie wrinkled her nose. "Are they having private time?"

Logan stifled a snort at everyone's shocked look.

Tristan put his coffee down. "Where did you learn that word, sweetie?"

"School," Maisie replied innocently. "Timmy said his daddies have lots of private time. He said he's not allowed to disturb them unless he's sick or the house is on fire."

Logan wheezed. James bit his lip hard, his shoulders trembling.

"Timmy sounds like a peach," Tristan said thinly.

Drake and Roman arrived just as Finn finished giving Logan a tour of his home and his artist studio. They followed the sounds of voices and laughter to a modern kitchen where everywhere had gathered, included a flushed Elijah and a smug Carter. Wyatt served them mulled wine from a punch bowl while Izzy placed a paper hat on their heads.

"Now you're officially part of the gang," she told Logan with a smile.

Logan touched his hat. "I'm honored." He raised an eyebrow as he observed Izzy and the men gathered in the kitchen. "So, are we changing our name to the Terrible Fifteen?"

Hunter's face fell. "That's an awful name."

"I don't know." Theo shrugged. "I kinda like it."

"Let's vote on it," Roman suggested. "Since it's Christmas, the winner gets a no-questions-asked wish from the losers."

Drake's expression turned predatory. "Does he, now?"

Roman's ears reddened at his lover's hot stare.

Logan stole a glance at Miles. Miles's face was relaxed in a genuine smile as he sat watching the couple, Maisie on his lap.

It seems he's really over Drake.

The knot in Logan's belly loosened. Though he'd acted nonchalant when he'd told Miles he knew about his secret crush on Drake, he hadn't been able to completely quell the green monster lurking inside him.

He's mine now.

Logan had never thought of himself as having a possessive nature. Not until he met Miles. He masked a grimace.

I wonder if he'll freak out if he could hear my thoughts right now.

Logan was distracted by Izzy's dry words.

"How about you guys stop flirting in front of the kid?" Izzy was telling Drake and Roman.

Maisie stared at Drake and Roman in open fascination. "Are Uncle Drake and Uncle Roman going to do smoochies too?" she asked Miles eagerly.

"I hope not," Miles said tartly.

Maisie's crestfallen expression made everyone chuckle.

The rest of the afternoon and evening passed in a blur of easy conversation and laughter. They played board games after dinner while Maisie slept on a couch with the two dogs and didn't go to bed until late.

Logan sighed contentedly as he took Miles into his arms. They were lying on the sofa bed in Finn's studio, the night sky bright with stars where it was visible through the glass roof above their heads.

"Today was fun."

"Yeah. I'm glad we came." Miles laid his head on Logan's chest and sighed. "Thanks for being here with me."

Warmth flooded Logan's heart. His stomach contracted on a wave of desire.

"Miles?"

"Yeah?"

"I really want to make love to you right now."

Miles sucked in air and lifted his head. "We can't!"

Logan laughed at his shocked look and kissed the tip of his nose. "Alright, I won't, Mr. Prude. But all bets are off once we get home." He ran a hand down Miles's back and squeezed his butt. "You know, this studio is pretty isolated from the rest of the house," he whispered seductively. "I'm sure we can...find something else to do that'll be just as fun."

Miles flushed and bit his lip. "You're terrible."

His swelling cock probed Logan's thigh. Logan grinned. "I think your dick likes that idea."

Their heavy breathing filled the studio as they used their hands and their mouths to pleasure each other. They soon collapsed in a sated heap and fell into a deep sleep, their arms and legs wrapped around one another.

CHAPTER TWENTY-FIVE

CHRISTMAS MORNING FOUND THE VALLEY AND THE forest covered in a thick blanket of snow.

Alex stared out of the living room wall. "Wow, it's really coming down hard out there."

Miles followed his gaze. They were opening their gifts over coffee and a light breakfast, Maisie giggling and squealing excitedly as she unwrapped the bevy of fun things Santa had brought her.

The terrace had already disappeared under several inches of snow. Ice floated in the creek below.

Tristan checked his phone and frowned. "The forecast says an unexpected storm is sweeping in from the east."

By the time they finished the feast Elijah and Wyatt prepared for lunch and retired to the living room to watch Christmas movies, a fierce wind was howling outside.

Miles shivered as he stared at the treetops bowing in the storm. "I'm glad we're staying in."

Logan squeezed his arms around him where they sat on the floor next to the fire, their backs against a couch. "So am I."

His cell vibrated.

Logan frowned and checked the caller ID before answering. "Lucy? What's wrong?" His face tightened as he listened.

Unease coiled inside Miles. His heart sank at Logan's next words.

"Alright, I'll be there as soon as I can," Logan said stiffly.

"Logan?" Miles murmured after he disconnected.

Logan met his worried gaze. "A dog fell through the ice. Her owner just called Lucy. They're on their way to the practice."

Miles's stomach plummeted. He glanced outside. "You're going there in this storm?"

"He's right." Izzy furrowed her brow. "I doubt the town has had time to plow the mountain roads. They'll be treacherous."

Logan kissed Miles's temple. "I'll be careful."

Finn rose to his feet. "I have snow chains that'll fit your pickup."

"I'll help you guys put them on," Drake said.

Miles watched worriedly from the doorway as Finn and Drake kitted Logan's tires with the chains, the snow coming down so hard it piled on their heads and coats within minutes.

Logan got in and waved at Miles as he reversed. "I'll be back soon."

"Call me when you get to the practice!" Miles shouted.

Logan nodded and closed the window.

Pepper whined anxiously by Miles's feet. Miles picked the hound up and hugged her to his chest as they watched Logan drive off.

Miles was in the kitchen when his cell rang an hour later.

He almost dropped his phone as he yanked it out of his pocket.

"There, you see," Izzy said with a smile. She placed a coffee in front of him. "He got there okay."

Miles recognized Logan's practice number. He took the call, his hand trembling with the relief surging through him.

But it wasn't Logan who'd called.

"Miles?"

Miles stiffened. "Lucy?"

"I'm at the practice. Is Logan still with you?"

Acid burned the back of Miles's throat. "He left an hour ago."

Lucy inhaled sharply. "But he's—he's not here!"

"Miles?" Izzy was staring at him anxiously. "What's wrong? You've gone as white as a sheet."

Blood pounded in Miles's head, the fear clutching his heart so fierce he felt like he was dying. Lucy's panicked voice echoed from the phone speaker as his hand fell limply on his lap. He stared blindly at Izzy.

"Logan hasn't reached the practice," he whispered numbly.

Horror rounded Izzy's eyes. She moved past him

and dashed out of the kitchen. She returned with the others.

"I have another set of snow chains." Finn frowned at Drake. "They'll fit my Jeep and yours."

"Mine is geared for this kind of weather," Drake said in a hard voice.

Finn hesitated before nodding.

Miles swallowed, his gaze swinging between them. "What are you saying?"

"We're going to find Logan." Determination tightened Drake's jaw. He glanced at Izzy, who was calling emergency services as she paced the kitchen. "It might take forever until they find him. Besides, they'll be running a skeleton crew today. At least we know the route Logan took."

Miles shuddered and sagged. He bit his lip, trying not to let panic overwhelm him. Roman pressed a comforting hand on his shoulder.

"We should bring Pepper," Tristan said. "She'll probably sense Logan if we get close enough to where he is."

"Let's get those snow chains on your Jeep," Hunter told Drake grimly.

Drake, Tristan, Wyatt, Hunter, and Miles got in the vehicle minutes later. Izzy and Roman came out with blankets and a couple of hot flasks while Alex brought them an emergency kit.

"Be careful," Izzy mumbled. "All of you."

Miles registered her haggard look for the first time. Guilt twisted his belly.

Is this what it was like for Izzy when she heard about our accident? Did she feel the same suffocating terror and helplessness I'm feeling right now?!

Every moment Miles had spent with Logan flashed before his eyes as Drake headed out of Finn's estate and slowly made his way through the blizzard sweeping across the valley surrounding Twilight Falls. Every kiss. Every touch. Every smile. Every gasp of pleasure.

Every loving look.

Miles blinked. *I love him. I love Logan!*

He didn't realize he was crying until Hunter wrapped an arm around his shoulders and hugged him to his chest.

"It will okay," Hunter said in Miles's hair, his voice steady and strong. "We'll find him."

They'd just reached the bottom of the mountain when Pepper woofed. Drake gently tapped on the brakes. Pepper put her forepaws on the dashboard where she sat on Tristan's lap. She started barking agitatedly.

"There!" Wyatt shouted.

Miles stared frantically to where he pointed. His eyes widened. His breath hitched.

Something big had plowed through the snowdrifts that had piled on the verge. The track disappeared between the trees and down a bank.

Drake parked the Jeep on the side of the road and put hazard triangles around the vehicle while Miles and the others made their way to the edge of the embankment.

A choked sound left Miles.

"Shit!" Tristan swore.

Wyatt grabbed his cell and dialed emergency services.

Logan's pickup was lying on its side at the bottom of an incline, near a stream. The driver's door was facing the sky and was badly dented, the paintwork scraped and damaged. A beat-up Cadillac sat in the water a few feet from the pickup, hood buckled and steam escaping from the heated engine as snow piled on top of it.

Fear sapped the strength from Miles's legs. His knees buckled.

Hunter cursed and caught him around the waist.

It was clear the car had crashed into Logan's pickup and carried it over the edge of the road.

Pepper jumped out of Tristan's arms and scampered down the slope, her low woofs echoing against the snow laden trees. They followed, Hunter retracing his steps swiftly to grab the blankets and hot flasks while Drake took a crowbar out of the trunk of his Jeep.

Miles fell on his knees when they reached Logan's pickup. He peered through the chipped windshield, his heart slamming against his ribs.

A moan tumbled from his lips. "No!"

Logan hung limply in his seat, his belt locked tightly around his chest and hips. A trail of blood had congealed on his temple.

He was pale and motionless.

"Let me take a look," Drake said urgently. He looked in at Logan and shuddered. "He's breathing, Miles." He clutched Miles's shoulder. "He's still alive!"

Tears blurred Miles's eyes.

"Let's get this door open," Drake told Tristan grimly.

They climbed on the pickup and used the crowbar to try and pry the damaged door free. Wyatt and Hunter made their way over to the other vehicle.

"They're alive too!" Wyatt shouted a moment later.

He and Hunter helped a dazed, elderly couple out of the car. The woman's leg looked like it was broken and the man had a nasty injury to his head.

Miles flinched and looked around when the pickup door clattered onto the snow covered bank. He scrambled up beside Drake and reached for Logan.

"Don't!" Drake grabbed his hand. "He hurt his head. It's dangerous to move him."

Miles's nails dug into his palm as he slowly retracted his arm.

Drake carefully checked the pulse in Logan's throat. He sighed, his shoulders sagging.

"Strong and steady," he murmured. "I think he's just knocked out."

They covered Logan with a couple of blankets. Tristan helped Miles down onto the ground and gave Pepper to him. The dog whined and fretted in Miles's arms.

The twenty minutes it took for the first ambulance and fire truck to reach them were the longest of Miles's life. He spent every second of them sending a silent prayer to whoever God happened to be listening as he gazed blindly at Logan through the broken windshield.

CHAPTER TWENTY-SIX

Logan woke up with a splitting headache. He opened his eyes and groaned when bright light pierced his vision.

His chest hurt and his mouth felt like something had died inside it.

Someone sucked air close by. "You're awake."

Logan realized he was lying in a hospital bed. He looked around carefully.

Drake was rising from one of the chairs in the room.

Lucy startled awake beside him. Tears pooled in her eyes when she saw Logan. Her face crumpled.

"I'm so sorry!"

Logan's last memory flitted before his eyes. His pulse quickened.

He recalled rounding a bend as he neared the foot of the mountain and headlights coming at him from the other side of the road. He swallowed.

That's right. I was in an accident!

"It wasn't your fault, Lucy," Logan managed. He sat slowly and winced.

"You're bruised pretty badly." Drake frowned and headed for the door. "I'll go get a nurse."

"Where's Miles?" Logan mumbled.

A muscle jumped in Drake's jawline as he stopped in the doorway. He looked at Logan over his shoulder, his expression strangely shuttered.

"He's in the waiting room with the others."

Logan puzzled over his stilted tone as he disappeared.

"How's the dog you called about?" he asked Lucy.

"She's fine." Her expression remained haunted. "I shouldn't have called you." Lucy dropped her face in her hands, her shoulders trembling. "I should have just handled it myself. I feel so guilty that I put you and Miles through this."

Logan looked out of the window. The snowstorm had abated. What he could see of the landscape was covered in fresh, white snow.

"What day is it?"

"December twenty-eighth," Lucy mumbled.

Logan's stomach plummeted. "I was out for two days?!" he said hoarsely.

A nurse turned up before Lucy could reply, Drake trailing in her steps. Izzy and Alex weren't far behind.

The nurse checked Logan over and left to report his status to the doctors.

"I'm so glad you're okay." Izzy sat on the bed and grasped Logan's fingers with a trembling hand. There were dark circles under her eyes. "When Wyatt told me they'd found you, my heart almost stopped."

Logan reeled. "What? Wyatt found me?"

Izzy glanced at Drake and Alex before meeting Logan's stunned gaze.

"Lucy called Miles and said you hadn't made it to the practice. Drake, Tristan, Wyatt, Hunter, and Miles went looking for you with Pepper. They found your pickup and the car that crashed into you."

"Miles." Panic squeezed Logan's chest all of a sudden. He could only imagine what must have gone through Miles's mind when he'd seen that Logan had been in an accident. "Where is he?!"

"He's—" Izzy stopped and chewed her lip.

"I'll, er, go get a drink," Lucy murmured awkwardly. She rose and left.

Alex blew out a heavy sigh after she disappeared. He ran a hand through his hair. "Your boyfriend's being a coward," he told Logan in a tired voice.

"Alex," Izzy protested.

"Alex isn't wrong, Izzy," Drake said sternly. "If anyone has the right to react the way Miles is doing, it's you. This is the second time you've had to live through something like this."

Izzy paled. She looked down at the bedsheets, her lower lip trembling. "That's why I know what it's like." Her voice broke. "I know what he's going through right now."

Drake cursed and came over to wrap his arms around her.

Blood pounded in Logan's veins. "Izzy, can I have your phone?"

Izzy wiped her eyes with the back of a hand and gave him a puzzled look. "Why?"

"I'm going to call him."

Izzy blinked. "Oh." She dug inside the pocket of her jacket and passed Logan her cell.

Logan's chest tightened as he dialed Miles's number.

Miles answered on the first ring. "Izzy? Is everything okay?!"

Air whooshed out of Logan at Miles's voice.

He sounds terrified.

"It's me," Logan whispered.

Miles drew a sharp breath.

"I'm okay, Miles. So please, let me see you," Logan begged softly.

"I—" A sob left Miles. "I can't. I'm—I'm too scared."

Logan took a shaky breath. "What are you scared of, Miles?"

"That you'll disappear right before me. That you'll— that you'll die!"

Logan squeezed his eyes shut, his stomach in knots. "I *will* die one day, Miles."

A tortured sound left Miles.

"But I hope it will be a long, long time from now," Logan continued, determination strengthening his voice. "I have a whole lifetime to spend with you first, Miles Martinez. A lifetime of good mornings and goodnights. Of kisses and making love. Of fighting and making up." A shudder shook him. "A lifetime being grateful that I found you. I love you, Miles."

Miles's crying echoed in Logan's ear.

Izzy sniffed and blubbered. Alex passed her a tissue, his own eyes glittering. Drake patted their backs.

But whatever Logan said to Miles and however much he pleaded with him, he refused to come see Logan. Logan's heart weighed heavily in his chest when he was discharged from the hospital the next afternoon, the doctor leaving him with strict instructions to convalesce for the next two weeks.

Lucy had called that morning. She'd rebooked all his routine appointments and referred the urgent surgeries they'd planned to do to other vets on their roster.

Tristan and Wyatt were waiting for Logan when he came out of the main entrance. They'd arranged to take him home.

"I'm sorry about Miles," Wyatt muttered as he climbed in the driver's seat of his SUV.

"There's no need to apologize, Wyatt." Logan sighed where he sat in the backseat. "If anything, I should be thanking you guys. I'm pretty sure you saved that old couple. They would have died from hypothermia if you hadn't found us." He grimaced. "And I'd probably be much worse off."

The daughter of the man and woman who had crashed into Logan had visited and apologized profusely on behalf of her bedridden parents stuck on another ward in the building. She'd banned them from driving their car when the weather was bad, but they'd insisted on going to see an old friend of theirs on Christmas Day. She promised to get their insurance company to process the paperwork related to the incident as quickly as possible before she left.

Tristan's voice jolted Logan out of his glum thoughts.

"Miles was the one stuck inside a pickup when we had our accident. It was…pretty damn horrible to watch." He met Logan's stare in the rearview mirror as Wyatt drove out of the hospital parking lot. "We were there for one another then. We'll be here for you and Miles."

Logan's chest tightened with emotion.

Miles's place was dark when Wyatt pulled up outside Logan's house.

"He's staying with Drake and Roman," Tristan explained at his crestfallen expression.

"Oh." Logan couldn't stop his stomach from sinking. He'd been hoping to go over and confront Miles. He was certain Miles would come around if they saw one other.

I want to touch him and kiss him so bad.

"Don't worry." Lines wrinkled Wyatt's brow. "Reinforcements will be here soon."

Logan stared. "What do you mean?"

Wyatt and Tristan exchanged a secretive look.

"Let's just say Miles's biggest champion will be back in Twilight Falls in two days," Tristan muttered.

CHAPTER TWENTY-SEVEN

MILES SAT ON THE SWING ON THE REAR VERANDA OF Roman and Drake's home. He tugged the blanket around his shoulders and clutched the hot drink in his hands as he gazed blindly at the covered swimming pool, and the garden and guest house beyond.

The Strickland Estate had a peculiar reputation in Twilight Falls. Once the property of an eccentric millionaire, it had laid empty for decades before Roman had finally bought it at the end of summer. Despite being told the place was haunted, the rockstar had signed on the dotted line two months after he'd first seen the place.

From what Miles had learned, Drake had had his eye on the Strickland Estate for even longer and had been annoyed as hell when Roman had snatched it from under his nose weeks before he'd been considering putting an offer on the property himself. It had led to a brief war of attrition between the pair before they had given in to the attraction burning between them.

Miles looked over his shoulder at the lovingly restored colonial mansion.

I can see why both Drake and Roman fell in love with this place.

Roman came out the back door. "Hey." He joined Miles on the swing.

"How's the song coming along?" Miles said lightly.

Roman smiled faintly. "It's finished."

A comfortable silence fell between them.

"Trauma is a funny thing." Roman stared out over the snowy garden. "Some days, it leaves you alone. Other days, it eats you alive until you have nowhere to run and you want to curl in on yourself and die."

Miles's stomach lurched. He stared dazedly at Roman.

The rockstar met his shocked gaze. "I take it my bad boy reputation never made it to your ears?"

Miles shook his head, his pulse racing. He recognized the darkness in the depths of Roman's gaze. He could see the same darkness in his own eyes every single day since Logan's accident.

The memory of the moment he'd seen Logan's smashed up pickup and the hours Logan had laid unconscious in the hospital had dragged him in a pit of despair from which he feared he would never emerge.

It was worse than what he'd felt when he'd woken up from his coma.

Much, much worse.

"I spent my late teens and a significant part of my

twenties high on drugs and alcohol." Roman folded his legs up on the swing and hugged his knees. "I was in a dark place for a long, long time. I probably would have died from an overdose if it hadn't been for James and Crazyknot looking out for me." His expression grew haunted.

Miles swallowed, almost afraid to ask the question. "What—what happened to you?"

"My mom left me and my twin sister when we were little." Roman's voice was dead. "Our father was a drunk and a gambler. He also loved taking out his anger on us. He used to beat us, lock us in a closet, and starve us. One day, after we turned fifteen, my sister went home early from school and slit her wrist with a kitchen knife."

Miles gasped. His vision blurred.

Roman rested his chin on his knees and reached over to wipe the tear coursing down Miles's cheek, his mouth tilted in a soft smile. "Why are you crying, silly?"

"Because—because that's just horrible!" Miles's breath hitched.

Roman inched closer and wrapped an arm around Miles. "Trauma *is* horrible, Miles. But it doesn't mean you have to let it crush you." He hesitated. "I still have bad days. But they are months apart now, instead of weeks. And I'm pretty sure they will disappear, one day." His tone lightened. "I have Drake to thank for that. And James and my friends." He chuckled. "But Drake definitely does more to make me forget."

Miles gave him a quizzical look.

"The best pick me up when you're down is sex,"

Roman said bluntly. "I usually ask Drake to fuck me senseless until I can't spare a single thought for my worries."

Miles choked on air. Roman laughed.

The back door opened.

Drake came out on the veranda, a strange expression on his face.

"Miles, you have a visitor."

Miles's legs went weak. *Logan!*

But it wasn't Logan who emerged from Roman and Drake's home.

"Miles Martinez, I need to have a word with you," Elaine said with a stern look on her normally kind face.

Miles opened and closed his mouth soundlessly. He jumped to his feet.

"*Mom?!*" he finally squeaked. "What are you doing here? You were supposed to come home next week!"

"I took an early flight." Elaine closed the distance to Miles and touched his cheek, her hand gentle despite her steely voice. "What's this I hear about my son being a chicken?"

Miles shot an accusing look at Drake.

Drake shrugged. "Hey, I'm not the one who called her."

"Let me guess?" Miles grumbled. "It was Izzy."

"Wrong," Elaine snapped. "It was Hunter."

Drake raised an eyebrow. "Hunter tattled?"

"Like the proverbial canary," Elaine said drily. "That child didn't pause for breath."

Miles's heart thundered against his ribs. "What—what did Hunter say to you?"

Elaine's expression softened a little. "That you are madly in love. That the man you care for was in an accident. And that the thought of losing him has you so scared you'd rather not see him for fear it would break your heart."

Emotion clogged Miles's throat.

"How about we do this inside?" Roman suggested gently.

They went in the house. Drake made them all hot drinks and joined them at the kitchen island.

Elaine grasped Miles's hand and gazed at him steadily. "The days after your accident were the darkest of my life. I had already lost your father. The thought of losing you nearly drove me mad with pain." She squeezed Miles's fingers, her eyes brimming with emotion. "You know who got me through that awful, awful time?"

Miles shook his head, his chest tight.

"It was Izzy." Elaine reached over to take Drake's hand. "And Drake. And Hunter. And every one of those precious boys who loved you more than you could ever have known. They were the pillars that kept me standing. The glue that stuck me together on the days I fell apart. They became my strength and eventually pulled me out of the dark place where I had fallen."

Drake's face grew flushed. Miles's vision blurred with fresh tears.

"It's okay to be afraid, Miles," Elaine said tenderly. "But you aren't alone. You have me and Izzy and the Terrible Seven and—"

"Awesome Fifteen," Roman mumbled.

Elaine blinked. "What?"

"We changed the name of the gang at Christmas," Drake explained. "Logan came up with it."

"Oh." Elaine tilted her head to the side. "I like it. Logan sounds like a smart guy." She turned to Miles. "As I was saying, we're all here for you. We have *always* been here for you." Elaine narrowed her eyes. "So, make your mamma proud and go claim your man, Miles Martinez."

CHAPTER TWENTY-EIGHT

Logan sighed for what felt like the hundredth time. Pepper looked up where she was lying by his feet in the den. She whined softly.

"I know," Logan murmured. "I miss Miles and Blue too."

Pepper jumped on the couch and licked his face before plopping down on his lap. They were watching the fire crackling in the hearth when the doorbell rang.

Pepper raised her head. An excited woof left her.

She jumped on the floor and darted out of the room.

Logan's pulse quickened. He rose and went out in the hall.

A familiar figure was outlined through the frosted glass in the door.

Miles!

Logan stormed inside the foyer and pulled his front door open, Pepper huffing animatedly beside him.

Blue bolted inside the house and yipped wildly as he jumped around Pepper.

Miles wasn't alone. Logan stared at the woman standing beside his pale-faced lover.

She smiled at him warmly. "Hi, Logan. I'm Elaine Martinez, Miles's mom."

Logan's heart thudded against his ribs. He swallowed. "Hello, Mrs. Martinez." His gaze shifted to Miles. "Hey."

Elaine put a hand to Miles back and pushed him forward. "Go on."

Some color returned to Miles's face. "I—I'm sorry. I should have—!"

Logan closed the distance to him, clutched his face, and took his mouth in a passionate kiss. Miles gasped before melting against him, his arms rising to loop tightly around Logan's neck.

Elaine cleared her throat discreetly a moment later.

Logan reluctantly lifted his mouth off Miles. Miles blinked at him dazedly before touching his swollen lips, his cheeks rosy and his eyes bright.

Logan gave Elaine a sheepish look. "I'm, er, sorry."

Elaine chuckled. "Don't be. I'm glad to see how much you love and treasure my son. How about I give you boys some time?" Mischief brightened her eyes. "On second thought, I'll see you for breakfast tomorrow."

"Mom!" Miles mumbled, mortified.

Elaine grinned. "Happy New Year." She kissed Miles and Logan on the cheek and looked at Blue. "Come on, Blue." Elaine leaned down and scratched Pepper under the chin. "You must be Pepper. Want to come and spend some time with me?"

Logan patted Pepper's head. "Go on."

Pepper hesitated before following Elaine and Blue across the porch and down the steps.

Logan closed the front door and turned to look at Miles. His stomach clenched as he studied his beautiful face and the circles under his eyes.

"Come here."

Miles flew into his arms.

They kissed with wild abandon, their hands moving all over one another, as if they couldn't quite believe that they were finally together.

"I'm sorry I was such a coward," Miles mumbled against Logan's lips. "I love you, Logan. I want to be with you now and forever more."

Logan's heart raced as he stared into Miles's glittering eyes and saw the love and trust shining brightly in his gaze.

"I love you so much, Miles."

He took his mouth in a slow, reverent kiss full of promise. Miles shivered, his fingers twitching on Logan's back. Desire coiled through Logan and thickened his cock.

Miles made a soft sound when Logan's erection nudged his thigh.

Logan let go of Miles's lips, took his hand, and led his upstairs to his bedroom, blood pounding in his veins and dick.

Miles's eyes rounded when he saw the freestanding

mirror opposite the foot of the bed. "When did you get that?"

Logan kissed and nibbled on his knuckles as he guided him across the floor. "I ordered it after we slept together for the first time. It came yesterday." He tugged Miles into his arms and palmed his butt. "Remember what I said I wanted to do?"

Miles shivered and bit his lip before nodding.

"Good." Logan ducked his head and claimed the pulse beating frantically at the base of Miles's throat with hot lips. "Because I'm going to fulfil every filthy fantasy I've ever had about you, so you'd better be prepared, Miles Martinez," he murmured against his trembling skin.

Miles moaned.

They hurriedly stripped out their clothes, their mouths meeting again and again in feverish kisses, their hands touching and stroking heated skin and rock hard flesh.

Logan pushed Miles down on the bed, yanked his waist so he was lying on the edge of the mattress with his legs over the side, and spread his thighs open.

Miles pushed up on his elbows and panted as he watched Logan kneel between his legs. Logan eyed Miles's flushed erection before closing his hand around the root of his shaft.

A guttural sound escaped Miles when Logan opened his mouth wide and took him in to the back of his throat.

Miles clutched his fingers in Logan's hair and fell back on the sheets as Logan started blowing him hard and deep. He bent his knees, pressed his heels on the bed, and started undulating his lower body, his soft cries filling Logan's ears as he rolled his hips and thrust his cock in and out of Logan's eager mouth.

He came on a sob that raised the hairs on Logan's nape. Logan swallowed Miles's hot cum, relishing his salty taste and musky scent. He wrapped his tongue around Miles's twitching member and dragged his lips along his length before he let go.

Miles collapsed on the bed, his chest shuddering and his belly contracting as the last waves of his orgasm washed through his body.

Logan rose, took condoms and a bottle of lube from the bedside drawer, and dropped them on the bed. He climbed on the mattress, his erection so hard he wasn't sure how he hadn't exploded yet.

Miles blinked when Logan maneuvered him into the middle of the bed. Color stained his cheekbones at the sight of Logan's cock.

"Let me suck you," he breathed.

Logan clenched his jaw. "I won't last long if you do that."

A hiss escaped his gritted teeth when Miles touched his straining erection lightly and fondled his balls.

"We have all night," Miles said huskily. "You can come inside me however much you want, Logan."

Logan cursed at the filthy invitation. He lay on his back and guided Miles so he straddled his body and faced the foot of the bed and the mirror. Excitement rounded Miles's pupils when he found himself positioned above Logan's cock. He grasped Logan's cock and licked the tip, only to hiss when Logan parted his ass cheeks and blew out a breath on his twitching pucker.

Logan flicked his tongue across Miles's tight folds.

"Logan!" Miles shouted, shocked.

"Yes, Miles?" Logan teased Miles with his tongue again.

"*Ah!*" Miles arched his back, his cock swelling where it bobbed between his legs. "That—!"

Logan slapped Miles's butt lightly, making his gasp and bite his lip. "I believe the words you're looking for are *'That feels good'*, Mr. Martinez. Now, how about you suck my cock while I eat this pretty little hole of yours?"

Miles shuddered and panted as Logan spread him open with his thumbs and circled his rim with his wicked tongue. He started licking and sucking Logan's cock, his gasps and moans making Logan groan as the sounds reverberated through his aching flesh.

It didn't take long for Logan to come in Miles's mouth. He furrowed his tongue and pierced Miles's loose pucker over and over again as he grunted and groaned, his hand reaching up between Miles's legs to stroke his erection.

Miles let go of Logan's twitching dick and dropped his head, his eyes glazed and his lips open on sultry sounds as Logan worked his body toward his next orgasm. He came with sweet violence, his ass pulsing sinfully against Logan's mouth as he writhed and punched his hips, his cock ejaculating cum all over Logan's chest and belly.

Logan's heart thrummed wildly at the sight, Miles's hoarse grunts echoing in his ears. He moved out from under Miles, tugged his turgid flesh to a fresh erection, and was reaching for a condom when Miles grabbed his hand.

"No." Miles stared at him feverishly where he braced on all fours, his body trembling from the pleasure he'd just received. "I want to feel all of you, Logan. I want you to take me raw."

A buzzing sounded in Logan's skull. "Are you sure?"

"Yes." Miles held his dazed gaze. "Take me the way you want to."

Logan shuddered. Miles was giving him permission to do something he'd only ever dreamt of doing. He'd never had bareback sex before, be it with a woman or a man. The thought had his cock twitching.

Logan knelt behind Miles, flicked the cap off the bottle of lube, and poured a generous amount on his hand and on Miles's pucker.

Miles shivered when Logan rubbed his folds and pressed his thumb inside him. Their gazes found the mirror. A thrilled hum left Miles's throat when Logan removed his thumb and slipped two fingers inside his passage.

Logan met Miles's hot stare as he finger fucked his slick hole. Miles's gaze locked on Logan's hand where it moved against his ass. He tugged his bottom lip between his teeth.

Logan smiled savagely. "Do you like what you see, Miles?" He inserted a third finger inside Miles.

Miles bit his lip and nodded, color painting red flags on his cheekbones.

His eyes were wild with lust.

Logan groaned at the sight. He worked Miles's entrance loose before taking his fingers out. Logan crowded Miles's back, hitched his hips up, and stretched his pucker open.

An animal grunt left him when he pressed his eager cock against Miles's hole. He rolled his hips and entered him.

"*Aaah!*" Miles hissed. His fingers clenched on the sheets and his head drooped.

Logan reached for Miles's hair and arched his neck up and back so he was looking in the mirror.

"Watch as I take you, Miles," he growled.

Miles whimpered, his feverish gaze arrowing in on where Logan's cock was slowly piercing him.

Logan shivered and squeezed his eyes shut at the silken heat of Miles's body. Having bareback sex with Miles was an experience he would never forget for as long as he lived.

Miles moaned wantonly when Logan punched through the inner ring guarding his passage and drove in to the hilt. The way his ass squeezed Logan's cock told him he'd found his sweet spot.

Logan stilled and opened his eyes. Miles's expression had him cursing.

"Move," Miles begged as he gazed at Logan's reflection in the mirror. "Fuck me, please!"

He cried out when Logan did just that, pulling out

and punching back in with enough force with make his body rock.

"Oh!" Miles's eyes nearly rolled into the back of his head. "*Aaaah!* Yes! Just like that!"

He swayed and gasped and moaned as Logan took him hard and fast.

Logan grunted at the sinful vision of their lovemaking in the mirror opposite the bed. Miles's expression was a study in sensual pleasure as he accepted everything Logan had to give him. Logan barely recognized his own face as he pounded Miles's ass, his motions rocking the bed with the force of his thrusts. He gritted his teeth and hissed and growled at the insane bolts of electricity shooting through his cock and radiating through his body.

Miles came on a harsh shout, his body anointing the sheets with his cum.

His convulsions tipped Logan over the edge of the cliff of pleasure he'd been skirting. Logan dropped his head back and sank his fingers in Miles's flesh as he ejaculated deep inside Miles's body, his hips punching his throbbing member fitfully against Miles's ass, slicking him up with his cum.

"Oh." Surprise widened Miles's eyes when Logan finally stopped moving. His chest heaved and sweat dripped down his face as he gazed blankly at Logan in their reflection. "You're still hard."

Logan swallowed, his pulse pounding violently. "That's never happened before," he said hoarsely.

Miles wriggled slightly. Logan groaned when he tentatively squeezed his steely cock.

"Wanna go again?" Miles said, his voice full of breathy anticipation.

Logan clutched his waist, pulled out, and punched his hungry cock inside his body.

Miles moaned deliciously and arched his back.

Logan leaned forward and trailed his lips down Miles's twitching spine. He worked a hand around Miles's body and took hold of his sensitive cock. Miles hissed.

Logan sank his teeth in Miles's shoulder and fucked and rubbed him to another screaming orgasm, the pleasure the act brought him so fierce his head fairly spun. They collapsed on the bed moments later, their bodies shuddering and damp with sweat.

Logan waited until he got his breath back before picking up Miles in his arms and carrying him into the bathroom so he could clean him up.

A sated sigh left Miles. His head lolled against Logan's chest.

"Love you," he mumbled.

Logan's heart ached with happiness as he ducked his head and kissed Miles.

EPILOGUE

Miles knocked on the door of Drake and Roman's bedroom.

"Come in," Roman called out.

Miles opened the door and walked inside the room. His breath caught.

Roman stood chewing his lip in front of a floor length mirror. He met Miles's gaze in the reflection. "Do I look okay?"

Miles smiled. "You look amazing."

"I told you you looked great," James grumbled.

James's duck egg blue outfit complemented Roman's gorgeous ivory wedding suit where he stood beside his best friend.

Miles walked over and tucked a dark red rose, thistle, and baby's breath boutonniere in the loop in Roman's jacket.

"Thank you," Roman mumbled. He pressed a hand

to his chest and squeezed his eyes shut. "God, I didn't think I'd be so nervous on my wedding day!"

James arched an eyebrow. "You know there's bet going on as to whether you're gonna faint when you walk down the aisle, right?"

Roman's eyes slammed open. Outrage painted rosy flags on his cheekbones. "Who the heck started that bet?!" He furrowed his brow. "It was Hunter, wasn't it?"

"Hmm." Miles scratched his nose awkwardly. "It was Logan, actually."

Roman opened and closed his mouth soundlessly. "That—that villain!" he blurted out.

James snorted. Miles bit his lip hard.

A knock came at the open door.

"You ready?" Tristan said. He looked wickedly handsome in a navy tux with a red boutonniere.

Roman inhaled shakily. "As ready as I'm going to be, I guess."

Miles, James, and Tristan accompanied Roman down the stairs and through the mansion.

Drake and Roman had decided to get married in their home.

It was more than big enough to hold the wedding and the reception and had the advantage of being hidden from the curious eyes of the hungry media.

A dry smile curved Miles's mouth.

Twilight Falls had been veritably infested with news vans in the past two weeks as journalists from all over the country tried to get a peek into the rockstar's private life and the venue where he was getting married. Since James had hired enough security to rival

Fort Knox, Miles doubted any reporter would get inside the estate.

Wyatt was waiting for them at the back door. He signaled to the wedding band before smiling at Roman. "You look incredible."

"Thank you," Roman whispered.

Miles's gaze dropped from Roman's ashen face to his trembling hands where he clutched his bouquet.

Roman flinched when Miles touched his shoulder.

"Drake is waiting for you at the end of that garden. He loves you and wants to be with you. So, don't be afraid, Roman." Miles kissed Roman's cheek. "Go claim the future you both want."

Roman's lower lip wobbled as he gazed at Miles. He sniffed and bobbed his head. James hooked his arm through Roman's elbow and guided him out of the mansion and down into the garden as the wedding march started playing.

Crazyknot was doing the honors, the band members smiling goofily as they watched their cherished friend walk down the white and red petal-strewn aisle between the rows of seats packing the lawn.

Drake stood waiting under a green wedding arch festooned with pale hydrangeas, delphiniums, and roses, Alex standing by his side. Drake's eyes gleamed and a dazzling smile curved his mouth at the sight of his soon-to-be husband.

Roman's face relaxed. He beamed back at Drake.

Miles and Tristan took their seats in the front row.

"Hey." Logan dropped a kiss on Miles's cheek and

studied Roman with a faint smile. "I see you managed to calm his nerves."

"James told him about the bet," Miles murmured.

Guilt danced across Logan's face.

"What bet?" Elaine asked quizzically on the other side of Miles.

Logan sighed and confessed the wager he had going with the other guys.

Elaine blinked. "Ooh, that's wicked." She patted Logan's cheek. "And totally what I've come to expect from my future son-in-law." Her tone turned amused. "Don't be surprised if Roman takes revenge at your own wedding. That child is a feisty little fox."

Logan blinked. Izzy snorted where she sat between Wyatt and Nathan.

Miles grinned.

Roman reached the arbor and took the hand Drake held out to him. They turned to face the minister officiating their wedding.

"Dearly beloved, we are gathered here today in the presence of family and friends to celebrate the joining of these two men in the unity of marriage."

Logan slipped his hand through Miles's as they watched Drake and Roman pronounce their vows. Miles squeezed his fingers, his heart content and his soul drenched in the happiness of this precious moment and the man he was sharing it with.

Logan leaned over and whispered softly in Miles's ear. "I love you, Miles."

Miles smiled and kissed Logan.

THE END

Have you read the Nights series yet? Find out if Gabe Anderson accepts Cam Sorvino's promise of one night of mindless pleasure to help him overcome his phobia of intimacy!

Get One Night (Nights 1) today

Turn the page to read an extract now!

ONE NIGHT (NIGHTS #1)
SPECIAL PREVIEW

CHAPTER ONE

What the hell am I doing here?

Gabe Anderson scanned the crowded club in the mirror opposite the bar before looking down into his scotch with a self-deprecating smile. This had seemed like such a great idea an hour ago, when he'd been staring at an empty weekend in an even emptier apartment.

Saron was located in a side alley, a short walk from Shinjuku's main club strip. Despite its somewhat shady location, the place oozed style.

Gabe had hesitated when he'd seen the suited doorman guarding the entrance and wondered if access was by invitation only. He only knew of *Saron* from overhearing his clients mention it a few nights ago. From what he'd made of their excited conversation, it was *the* place to hang out in Shinjuku if you were of a particular sexual inclination.

The doorman had checked Gabe over for all of three seconds before wordlessly unclipping the rope from the stanchions framing the steel doors. He had obviously passed some kind of test, though what it was he didn't know.

Beyond a foyer with a cloakroom manned by a male attendant who looked like he'd walked straight out of a *GQ* shoot were a set of shallow steps leading to a wide, sunken floor.

Despite the butterflies churning his stomach, Gabe had stopped and stared appreciatively at the decor. As a consultant for one of Chicago's biggest design firms, he could tell how much money had gone into giving *Saron* its unique look. The club was drowned in deep reds, dark purples, and rich earth tones. Scattered across the oak floor were Brazilian cherry wood tables and armchairs boasting plush velvet upholstery and satin cushions. Discrete booths dotted the walls and afforded privacy to those who needed it, although the muted lighting provided enough of that as it was. A polished mahogany counter with wine-red leather and walnut stools ran the length of the bar on the right.

At the far end of the room, a woman in a black cocktail dress stood on a raised podium. She was crooning a song in a sultry, deep voice, her eyes closed and her glossy ruby lips glistening in the mellow spotlight. Behind her, cymbals vibrated gently, a piano tinkled, and a saxophone hummed, the sounds somehow rising above the voices of the men packing the place.

It was as he'd made his way to the bar that Gabe had realized why the doorman had let him in. From the looks of the club's patrons, *Saron* catered exclusively to an upscale clientele. He was willing to bet a week's wages none of the suits in the place cost less than five hundred dollars.

"Ah, fresh meat."

Gabe froze in the act of sitting on a barstool, his gaze swinging up to meet a pair of amused green eyes on the other side of the mahogany counter.

"Excuse me?" he said stiffly.

The bartender, a striking blond in a slate, silk tuxedo vest and crisp white shirt, flashed him a grin.

"I've not seen you around these parts before. What will it be?"

Gabe swallowed, wondering whether the man had seen straight through him and grasped the reason he had come to *Saron.*

"What will what be?" he mumbled, unable to mask the apprehension in his voice.

The bartender pursed his lips and observed him with a shrewd expression before leaning across the counter.

"Relax," he murmured in Gabe's left ear. "I can tell it's your first time in a place like this. If you keep up that deer-in-the-headlights look you've got painted across that pretty face of yours, you're gonna be a target for every sleaze ball in this club. And, trust me, they might be wearing thousand-dollar ensembles, but some of these assholes are nothing but dirty pigs in suits."

An involuntary bark of laughter left Gabe's lips at the mental image the bartender's words had conjured. The sound carried along the counter, drawing stares.

The knot of tension that had been sitting between Gabe's shoulder blades ever since he ventured into Shinjuku eased as he smiled at the bartender.

"I've never been called pretty before."

The guy winked.

"Trust me, you're the hottest thing on legs in this place right now. Besides me, of course."

Gabe chuckled and ordered a scotch, his confidence boosted by the compliment.

Two months had passed since he'd relocated to Tokyo from Chicago. When his bosses had sprung the offer on Gabe in early spring, the chance of a fresh start in a place void of the dark memories that had plagued him for eight years was too much of an attractive proposition for him to reject. He'd left Chicago with two suitcases and five crates full of books and artwork, the only things he had to show after a decade in the city.

Though he had been prepared for the culture shock, life in Tokyo had still come as a surprise, albeit an invigorating one. He had always had an interest in the country and its intoxicating mix of traditional and contemporary customs ever since he made his first business trip to the Japanese branch of the firm four years ago.

Luckily, his new position suited him to a T. He had thrown himself into his first assignment with his usual drive and passion, leading the team under him to make good on a project, one which his predecessor had only made a half-assed attempt to complete. He had delivered on time, on budget, and on schedule, despite the nearly impossible deadline. The crazy hours and weekends he had put in had not gone unnoticed, and the praise lavished on his team at the grand opening of their client's luxury hotel earlier that week was all the acknowledgment Gabe needed to realize he had made the right choice in moving to this city. The fact that the money he was making could easily afford him a two-bedroom condo in the exclusive neighborhood of Meguro didn't hurt, either.

Yet, despite having relocated thousands of miles to the other side of the world, his mind would not let go of the bite of his past. Which was why, when faced with the prospect of his first free weekend and the boxes he had yet to unpack, he had looked up *Saron*'s location on the spur of the moment and decided to take a gamble.

He had promised himself this move would not be just a fresh start for his mind, but for his body, too. That he would start taking risks in his personal life again. That he would not let the bastard who had made it impossible for him to ever have a satisfying physical relationship win.

Fifteen minutes into his first drink and Gabe wondered whether he had made a bad choice. So far, Ethan, the bartender, had helped him field a burly, yakuza-looking type with tattoos up the side of his neck, three old men with sweaty palms and bald patches, and a couple of young guys who looked barely past the legal age of drinking.

With his lean build, dark hair, and blue eyes, Gabe knew he was an attractive prospect. Add in that he was a foreigner and he was coming to the conclusion that he had become a beeline for all the men in the bar who wanted to make a conquest out of the white guy – a white notch in the proverbial bedpost. They all wanted to fuck him or be fucked by him.

A cynical half-smile twisted his lips at that thought. If only they knew.

He raised a hand to the back of his neck and rubbed the warm spot that had been bothering him for a while. Something made him look up from his drink then – call it instinct or that subconscious voice that warns of imminent danger. Movement in the mirror opposite the bar caught his gaze. Or, more precisely, a lack of it.

Stormy gray eyes pierced him from the other end of the club. They locked on him, a beam of light in the gloom. Transfixing him. Immobilizing him.

Gabe's breath caught in his throat, every muscle in his body tightening in fight-or-flight mode.

The man sat apart from the crowd, alone at a table that could have accommodated three, a tumbler full of dark liquid clasped casually in his left hand. His red silk tie was crooked, as if he had slipped a finger through the knot to loosen it. The top two buttons on his white shirt were open, revealing tan skin covering toned muscles and a hint of curls.

Gabe couldn't tell whether his hair was dark brown or dirty blond. It was hard to say in the dim light. What wasn't hard to see were the subtle and not-so-subtle stares the other men in the bar were giving the stranger.

With his stubbled face, smoldering looks, and what appeared to be an incredibly ripped body beneath a custom-tailored charcoal suit, the man looked like a king sitting on a throne, commanding a roomful of servants. Servants who appeared more than willing to either get fucked by him or fuck him if he so much as lifted his little finger.

And a man like that would not have to ask twice.

Envy and irritation flashed through Gabe at that thought, shattering the spell he found himself under. He broke eye contact, shocked by the feelings suddenly flooding him, and glared at his half-empty glass. It seemed to mock him, as if it were a reflection of his own life. A half-empty, broken shell. Incapable of touching someone or to be touched.

Gabe lifted the glass and downed the rest of the drink with an angry flick of his wrist. Fire singed his throat. He welcomed the burning sensation, hoping it would calm the pounding in his chest and the tightness in his belly and groin that told him his body had reacted to the stranger.

A full glass of scotch appeared next to his empty tumbler.

Gabe looked up at Ethan, puzzled.

A remorseful grimace flashed across the bartender's face. "Looks like we're no longer the two hottest bastards in this joint. Here, compliments of the King."

Gabe stared at the drink before slowly looking over his shoulder, his pulse picking up speed.

Gray Eyes raised his glass in a toast. A teasing smile played on his sculptured lips before he knocked back his drink.

You're kidding me.

Gabe tried to block out the heated tingle running across his skin at the stranger's cocky smirk and the way his powerful throat muscles worked when he swallowed. He turned to Ethan.

"That's his *actual* name?"

Ethan grunted. "Well, no. But the asshole sure acts like one."

There was movement in the mirror opposite Gabe.

Read One Night today

AFTERWORD

To all my friends who helped make this possible. You
know who you are.

To you, my readers. Thank you for reading Miles and
Logan's story. It's been an absolute pleasure and
privilege to bring you this sweet, hot, and incredible
sexy series. I would be grateful if you could leave a
review on Goodreads or on the store where you
purchased this book. Reviews help readers like you
find my books and I truly appreciate your honest
opinions about my stories.

Make sure to sign up to my store newsletter for special
deals on my books and new release alerts. Or you can
sign up to my author newsletter instead to get
upcoming release notifications, sneak peeks, and
giveaways.

BOOKS BY A.M. SALINGER

Ava Marie Salinger is the romance pen name of an Amazon bestselling author with a passion for writing addictive tales. Known for her action-packed and thrilling urban fantasy novels, she has expanded her repertoire with the introduction of the M/M urban fantasy romance series Fallen Messengers. Additionally, she has penned the scorching hot contemporary M/M romance series Nights and Twilight Falls as A.M. Salinger. When not immersed in her writing, Ava can be found curating inspiring music playlists, indulging in her love for nature, marveling at the latest gadgets, and savoring Chinese cuisine.

You can find all of Ava's books on her author store at shop.adstarrling.com